THE VOICE OF AN ANGEL
AND OTHER CHRISTMAS STORIES

THE VOICE
OF AN
ANGEL

AND OTHER CHRISTMAS STORIES

JOHN B. KEANE

MERCIER PRESS
PO Box 5, 5 French Church Street, Cork
16 Hume Street, Dublin 2

ISBN 1 85635 130 0

10 9 8 7 6 5 4 3 2 1

TO MAUREEN, DENIS AND SHANE

Printed in Ireland by Colour Books Ltd.

CONTENTS

THE VOICE OF AN ANGEL   7

A TASMANIAN BACKHANDER   23

CHRISTMAS NOSES   39

HIGH FIELDING   42

CHRISTMAS DIVERSION   52

THE WOMAN WHO HATED CHRISTMAS   65

PAIL BUT NOT WAN   78

THE GOOD CORNER BOY   81

SOMETHING DRASTIC   86

THE WOMAN WHO PASSED HERSELF OUT   101

THE BEST CHRISTMAS DINNER   122

THE LONG AND THE SHORT OF IT   140

CHRISTMAS ERUPTIONS   160

A LAST CHRISTMAS GIFT   163

THE URGING OF CHRISTMAS   185

The Voice

of an

Angel

A DRUNKEN SANTA CLAUS IS BETTER THAN no Santa Claus. I heard the remark in the kitchen of a neighbour, a genuinely frustrated mother of seven whose spouse had not returned as promised from an alcoholic excursion downtown where, as he maintained afterwards, he had been waylaid as he was about to return home by some whiskey-sodden companions from his childhood. Sensing that he would not return in time Maggie Cluney, that was the unfortunate mother's name, looked speculatively in my direction but after a brief inspection shook her head ruefully.

In those days I was a lathy, bony youngster about seven stones adrift, especially in the midriff, from an acceptable Santa Claus. The only other person in the kitchen over the age of ten was Maggie's sister Julie Josie who had earlier intimated that she was drunk which had given rise to the opening statement of our narrative.

After an hour's coaxing and two steaming hot whiskies we convinced her that nobody would fill the bill as she would. Drowsily, giddily she rose and inarticulately informed us that she was returning to her maidenly abode so that she could sleep off the excess spirits to which she was unaccustomed. Before she managed to stagger through the doorway we ushered the children out into the backyard and burdened her with the Santa Claus outfit from false beard to long boots, from tasselled headgear to vermilion great coat and finally the bag of gifts, one for every member of the household.

No great notice would be taken of her in the streets. She lived around the corner and besides there would be many other Santa Clauses abroad in various stages of inebriation but most would be sober and composed, conscious of the sacred missions with which they had been entrusted. Our particular one, Julie Josie, made her way homewards without mishap and also made it upstairs to her single bed where she fell instantly asleep.

Soon the room was filled with gentle snores, even and rhythmical, sonorous and richly feminine, snores that somehow suggested that deep in her subconscious was the need of a male companion who might take the sting out of the frost of life and fulfil her in a manner beyond the capacity of seasonal whiskey. In her sober everyday world she would never admit to any need whatsoever and often when questioned jocosely about her single state she would belittle all members of the opposite sex with a vehemence that made some believe she protested too much. For all that she was a good sister and a good aunt and an even better sister-in-law for she would always present herself *in loco parentis* whenever her sister gave birth and was a great favourite with her nephews, nieces and brother-in-law for the duration of her sister's confinement.

The night wore on until the ninth hour and it was precisely at this time that Julie Josie rose from her unassailable bed. She betook herself to a downstairs room where she donned the Christmas paraphernalia. She slung the bag of gifts across her shoulder and made her way to her sister's house where she was warmly received by her brother-in-law who insisted that she fortify herself with a drop of whiskey before the distribution of the gifts. Then and only then were the children called from the two small, happily-overcrowded bedrooms adjoining the kitchen.

The younger ones held back in awe whilst the older ones rushed forward to greet their beloved aunt, pretending as they did that she was really Santa Claus. Some people become imbued with the true spirit of Christmas when they don the red coat and Julie Josie was one of these. After the gifts were distributed they all sat around the fire, the children drinking lemonade and eating Christmas cake, the oldsters sipping whiskey and telling tales of bygone days when geese were really geese and Christmases were always white, when ghosts of loving ancestors whispered in the chimney and a tiny infant was turned away because there was no room at the inn.

Between the whiskey and the sentimental recall many a tear was shed. There were some in the neighbourhood who would say that Julie Josie shed enough tears at Christmas to float the *Titanic*. She was, truly, a sentimental soul, well meaning and generous to a fault. Several whiskies after her arrival she announced that it was time to go home. She refused all offers of assistance and even more adamantly refused to hand over her Christmas gear. She knew her way home didn't she! Wasn't she going back there now for the thousandth time and anyway what could possibly befall anybody at Christmas when men's hearts were full of goodness even if their bellies were full of beer!

She was, alas, drunker than she thought for she by-passed the corner which led to her house and went downtown in the general direction of the parish church. Mindless of her error she hummed happily to herself staggering to left and right and executing one daring stagger of record proportions which took her first backwards and then forwards, then hither and then thither, until she had travelled the best part of a hundred yards. Had her ever-increasing momentum not been arrested by the parish priest, Canon Coodle, she might well have wound up in the suburbs or even on the bank of the river which circled the town.

Luckily for Julie Josie the canon was a man of considerable girth and without any great strain he steadied the drunken representation of Christmas which wound up in his arms. Although a moderate imbiber himself he always made allowance for those who took a drop in excess on special occasions. He might shake his great, leonine head reproachfully when confronted by extreme cases and he might deliver the occasional sermon condemning the evil of over-indulgence to the detriment of the drunkard's wife and family but he never got carried away. If he had a fault, poor fellow, it was that he suffered from absent-mindedness. This was perhaps why he failed to identify the party who had collided with him. He presumed, and who would blame him, that the creature was male so he did what he always did with unidentified drunks. He directed this one to a warm room over the garage as he had all the others over the years, placed the now incoherent Julie Josie sideways on the bed and left her to her own devices convinced that she was a man and would sleep off the drink in a matter of hours before returning to wife and children.

As he tiptoed down the stairs the reassuring snores convinced him that all would be well in the course of time.

Earlier that night another intoxicated soul was chosen at random to fill the role of Santa Claus although he had never done so before, having neither chick nor child.

His name was Tom Winter and indeed it would have to be said that he looked wintry even in the height of summer for the poor fellow had a perpetually blue nose and was almost always a-shiver.

It was widely held by authoritative sources that he was generally emerging from a skite or booze or bender, call it what you will. Those who knew him best would explain that he only drank at weekends but that he drank so much during those particular days he spent the following five days recovering.

He was the proprietor of a small hardware business specialising in such commodities as sweeping brushes, mousetraps and chamber pots and, of course, nails, screws, hinges and what-have-you. He carried a considerable amount of his stock on his person. His waistcoat pockets, for instance, would be filled with shoelaces and his coat pockets with scissors, pen-knives and screwdrivers while his trousers pockets played host to less dangerous articles such as picture cord and pencil toppers. Whatever the customer needed, provided it wasn't a plough or a mowing machine, he would generally find it in a matter of moments on one of his shelves or in one of his pockets.

At six o'clock in the evening he closed his premises and

partook of a large cheese sandwich and a double gin before proceeding happily to his favourite tavern where it was his wont to indulge until closing time throughout the weekend and on festive occasions such as Christmas, Easter and Saint Patrick's Day or, of course, any other special occasion which might provide him with a break from routine.

Tom Winter, for all his wintry features, was a warm-hearted chap, gregarious in his own fashion so long as he didn't have to converse with more than two persons at the same time. He always bought his round and he frequently stood drinks to those who were less well off than himself or seemed that way.

Often it would occur to him that he drank too much and that he was wasting his life. His conscience would prick him from time to time and suggest that he might more profitably pursue some health-giving pursuits but, alas, when a weak-willed man wrestles with his conscience all the weight is on his side and the conscience is the victim of an unfair contest. So it was on Christmas Eve that Tom Winter found himself in the heel of the evening sitting on a high stool with a whiskey-sodden companion at either side of him.

Then a tall, thin, coatless man with his long, grey hair trailing behind his poll and ears dashed into the premises and allowed his gaze to wander from face to face. The obviously-demented creature shook his head in despair and then his eyes alighted upon Tom of the wintry dial. He raised an imperial finger which greatly alarmed Tom for he thought at first that the new arrival was either a ghost or a madman. After taking further stock Tom Winter recognised the intruder as a refugee from the northern part of the town, a sober hard-working chap with a large family and an even larger missus who kept him on his toes and who no doubt had dispatched him on some impossible mission on the very eve of Christmas.

Tom Winter's alarm grew even greater when he noticed that the hen-pecked unfortunate was beckoning him. It was as though he had been summoned by an ancient and pietistic patriarch of superhuman power for he found himself dismounting from his stool. For the first time in his life he began to feel how the twelve apostles felt when they were called from their various vocations to follow the man whose birthday was at hand. The grey-haired elder caught Tom Winter by the sleeve of his coat and led him out of doors. His companions were to say afterwards that Tom's normally wintry features had assumed a radiance that lighted up his head like an electric bulb. They would concede that it had been already moderately lighted by the intake of seven large gins and corresponding tonics but as he left the premises in the wake of the coatless messiah it seemed as though a halo was about to encircle his head and shoulders.

Outside in the night air the coatless one explained his predicament. His brother-in-law, at the best of times an unreliable sort, had promised to fill the role of Santa Claus and was now nowhere to be found. Would Tom Winter, out of the goodness of his heart, do the needful and don the red coat so that the poor man's seven children would continue to keep faith with Christmas!

Tom was about to decline when the coatless wretch fell to his knees and set up such a pitiful wailing that only a man with a heart of stone could continue to hold out. A stream of semi-coherent supplications that would bring tears from a cement block assailed Tom Winter's ears.

'If,' the kneeling figure was wailing, 'I don't come back home with some sort of Santa Claus she'll have my sacred life!'

Tom could only deduce that the grovelling wretch was referring to his outsize wife whose shrill voice could be heard above the wind and the rain during the long nights when fits of dissatisfaction soured her and she became discontented with her lot. She had been known to assault her terrified husband with rolling pins, cups, mugs and saucers and once with an iron kettle which necessitated the insertion of twenty-three stitches.

'Get up and behave like a man,' Tom Winter now adopted a wintry tone which had the effect of putting an end to the wailing. It was obvious that the poor creature was without backbone and if the right tone was adopted would obey any command. He struggled to his feet clutching wildly at Tom lest that worthy attempt to flee. Hope replaced the look of despair in his eyes as he babbled out his gratitude like a puling infant who has been lifted from the cradle.

On their weary way to the anguished fellow's abode Tom had the foresight to enquire if there was any gin on the premises.

'Gin!' came the echo.

'Yes!' Tom raised his voice and made several gin-swallowing motions.

'There may not be gin there now,' came the immediate and generous response, 'but there will be gin' and so saying the greatly-addled victim of wifely abuse dashed back into the pub and returned at once with a bottle of gin. Not only did he bring gin but under his other oxter was a bag containing several bottles of tonic water. Since he could not shake his hand for fear of damage to the bottles Tom Winter slapped him on the back in appreciation of his thoughtfulness.

When they arrived at the abode in question it was decided that they should use the back entrance so that the game might not be given away to the children. There, sure enough, hanging from a cobwebbed rafter was the Santa Claus coat, the Santa Claus hat and the Santa Claus beard. There were no long boots and for this Tom was grateful.

His companion acted as dresser and in jig time Tom Winter was indistinguishable, boots apart, from any other of the numerous Santa Clauses who roamed the country that night. It was agreed that the man of the house should first enter and announce that he had seen Santa Claus in the vicinity and that they should prepare some gin and tonic for his arrival.

A liberal glass of gin was poured and some tonic water added. The lady of the house whose name was Gladiola announced that she had developed a pain in the back as a result of the stress she had endured because of the absence of Santa Claus. She was presented with an equally liberal dollop of gin.

'Hush!' Gladiola raised a silencing hand and then entering fully into the spirit of the business called 'methinks I hear a step!'

Suddenly everybody from the youngest to the oldest was silent and indeed there was, sure enough, the sound of footsteps in the backyard. Then the back door of the kitchen opened and there entered with his tail in the air the family tomcat who had just returned from an amorous expedition to another part of town. He was followed by Santa Claus. The younger children hid behind their mother while the others crowded round their most welcome visitor and shook his hand and sang and danced and jumped atop the table while their father saw to it that their visitor was presented with his glass of gin into which, without delay, he made substantial inroads.

After the presents were distributed Tom Winter sat by the fire and was prevailed upon to accept another glass of gin.

'I will. I will,' he replied good-humouredly, 'but only if the lady of the house is having one too.'

The lady in question was more than agreeable and soon there was a half empty bottle where there had been a full one. Songs were sung and for all his wan, woebegone, winterish appearance Tom sang as warmly as any and since he was the proprietor of a soft mellow voice was much in demand as the night wore on.

For once the lady of the house did not resort to abusive language nor did she raise a hand in anger to her husband. Instead she addressed herself to the second gin bottle for which the man of the house had dispatched his oldest daughter. Did I say that he indulged in a glass or two himself? If I didn't let me say at once that he did and if I didn't say that he laughed and sang you may now take my word for it that he did and that he danced as well especially with the smaller members of the household.

The time passed happily and Tom Winter was obliged to admit to himself that he had never spent a better night. No sooner had the second gin bottle been emptied than the clock struck twelve. Declining all offers of tea and edibles Tom took his leave of the happy family in the fond hope that the pub he had vacated earlier in the night would be still manned by some of its staff for much as he enjoyed the household gin he, like all gin lovers, would, if asked, agree that there was no gin like the gin that comes across a bar counter. It is more natural for one thing and there is the unique atmosphere and there is the incomparable presence of drunken companions.

At the doorway, after he had made his goodbyes to the children, Tom Winter gave his word to Gladiola and her husband that he would do the needful without fail the following Christmas and during every Christmas thereafter while there was a gasp of life left in his body. Forgetting to disrobe, he turned his head towards his favourite watering hole. Although full to the gills with gin already he felt an insatiable desire to be reunited with the distinct camaraderie of that spot which had cheered him so often in the past. It is an astonishing aspect entirely of the toper's life that he most requires drink when he least needs it. No other thought now occupied Tom Winter's mind but the prospect of downing a glass of gin and tonic. Let the sot or the drunkard be mightily overburdened after his intake he will, nevertheless, always manage to find room for one more.

After many a skip and many a stagger he eventually arrived at his destination but there was, alas, no room at the inn, at least there was no room for Tom Winter so early on the morning of Christmas Day.

In the eye of the drinker there is no sight so sad as an empty public house or worse a public house which has retained its maximum number of clients and is not prepared, for the sake of comfort and safety, to admit anymore. He thought he heard the tinkling of glasses and chinking of coins in tills behind the closed doors, behind the shuttered windows. He had never in his life felt so lonely. It seemed as if the whole world had gone off and left him behind all alone.

Disconsolately he directed his steps towards his shop. Some time later, after it seemed that he had been walking all night, he realised that he had been going around in circles and it dawned on him that the reason for his aimless wandering might be because he really didn't want to go home. To begin with there was nobody there, no cat or no dog, not even a mouse for he had trapped them all in his many mousetraps. Again, more firmly this time, he directed his steps towards the shop but walk as he would he found himself no nearer his base.

Was there a superhuman force restraining him, keeping him away from calamity or was he so drunk that it was not within his power to focus himself properly? There came a time in his journeying when it seemed that he was destined to go on forever and then he fell into the benign arms of Canon Cornelius Coodle. At this stage he had been in the process of passing out.

'My poor fellow,' the Canon spoke gently as he dragged his stupefied find towards the garage and thence to the warm room upstairs where he deposited him upon the bed already occupied by the first Santa Claus. Canon Coodle had been surprised to see the first Santa Claus. He had totally forgotten but was relieved that no harm had come to the creature. He was quite taken by the fetching snores, not at all like those to which he was accustomed. He satisfied himself that the second Santa Claus was in no danger of suffocating and was pleased to acknowledge his first resounding snore. He stood for awhile at the head of the stairs, listening intently, a rapturous smile on his ancient and serene countenance. He reminded himself that he must tell his curates about this remarkable phenomenon in the morning but wait! What phenomenon! He racked his brains for several moments and then it came back to him. It was the harmonised snoring. Never in all his days had he heard anything so agreeable. It was as though the pair on the bed had been training together all their lives such was the perfect complimentary pitch of their joint renditions. He was reminded of a lyric by Thomas Moore:

> *Then we'll sing the wild song it once was such pleasure to hear*
> *When our voices commingling breathed like one on the ear.*

Surely this was a phenomenon or was it more! Was it a minor miracle, an act of homage to the creator on Christmas morning! He hurried downstairs for his tape recorder. Alas when he returned the snoring had ceased altogether and the pair now lay side by side breathing deeply and evenly, their white beards rising and falling as the air expelled itself from their lungs. Again he thought of Thomas Moore but resorted to parody in order to suit the occasion:

> *Where the storms that we feel in this wide world might cease*
> *And our hearts like thy snoring be mingled in peace.*

Raising his hand he breathed a blessing upon the contented pair before finally repairing to his bed and to the sleep he so richly deserved. As the night wore on the couple on the bed resorted occasionally to bouts of the melodious snoring heard earlier. Then came the dawn and Julie Josie stirred in her bed but did not open her eyes. Her head, surprisingly did not throb nor did her heart thump. She lay contented for awhile in the belief that she was in her own bed. When the snore erupted from somewhere beside her, some place too close for comfort, she too erupted and would have taken instant flight had she not become aware of her apparel.

She stood astonished looking down at the figure on the bed. She crept close to the recumbent form and gently removed the beard. She could scarcely believe her eyes. She knew Tom Winter well, had shopped with him, had always purchased her hardware wants from Tom and Tom alone and she recalled how at that very moment four different pictures hung from walls in her home, hung by Tom's picture cord from Tom's nails, which he had himself driven, and found to be good nails. She also recalled how her late father had purchased the hammer which had driven the nails.

She knew Tom Winter to be a gentle soul, a good-hearted chap who should not be judged on the strength of his wintry face alone. She decided to wake him. He raised himself slowly to his elbows and was surprised, to say the least, when he beheld Santa Claus standing by the bed.

'I'm sorry I didn't bring you anything,' the voice said and what a voice! It is surely the voice of an angel, Tom Winter told himself. He had never heard an angel's voice but he had imagined such a voice ringing in his ear one day and calling him to heaven if he was lucky, if he was very, very lucky. The voice he had just heard was the kind of voice which had called him in his more hopeful dreams.

'Did we sleep together?' he asked falteringly.

'Looks like it,' she answered with a laugh.

'In that case,' said Tom Winter solemnly, 'you must marry me. In fact,' he continued hardly believing himself to be possessed of such courage, 'I would marry you if we had never slept together. I have admired you many a time on the streets and in my humble shop which you have enhanced by your all too rare visits. Say you'll marry me and make my life into something glorious and good. Marry me and change my ways.'

She took his hand gently and was surprised to see that he was not in the least winterish at close quarters.

'We will talk about it some other time,' she whispered gently.

'I will give up the gin,' he promised, 'and never touch the accursed stuff again.'

'No need to give up all drink though,' came the pragmatic response. 'I firmly believe that a few beers now and then would stand you in better stead.' She looked at her watch and saw that it was twenty-five minutes to eleven.

'I'll have to hurry,' she said, 'if I'm not to miss mass.'

'So must I,' he told her.

'Have you any idea how we arrived here?' she asked. He shook his head. As they divested themselves of their Santa Claus coats she spoke again. 'There is something very strange about all this,' she ventured.

'I know. I know,' Tom Winter agreed. 'It's as though we were destined to be together. I mean why else would God join us together in this most unlikely place without either one of us knowing the first thing about it. Neither of us have any idea how we came to be here.'

They never would because the incident would have slipped Canon Coodle's mind after his breakfast and it would never surface again not even when he would marry them in the summer of the following year. He would baptise their children too in the years that followed and they would both live to see their children grow up and their grandchildren and even their great grandchildren so that it could be truly said of them that they both lived happily ever after.

A Tasmanian Backhander

'WHEN YOU MEET A BULLY,' ROGER WONSIT thrust his hands deep into his trousers pockets and surveyed the class of schoolboys before him, 'you must not allow yourself to be cowed and you must not take to your heels like a coward.'

He paused and allowed his injunctions to sink in before proceeding. He took a turn round the classroom, his head held high, a steely look in his grey eyes. His captive audience, for the most part boys of seven and eight years old, listened with mixed feelings as the famous ex-boxer clenched and un-clenched his fists.

Jonathan Cape, the second smallest boy in the class was glad he wasn't a bully. On the other hand he doubted if he would be able to stand his ground for long should a bully suddenly confront him. Roger Wonsit was going on.

'I,' he said and he paused for a longer period, 'have met many bullies in my time and I have dispatched them thus!' Here he feinted and thrust a straight left into the face of an imaginary bully before demolishing the scoundrel with a right cross.

'There are other methods,' he went on belligerently, 'but the most important thing is that you must never allow anything or anybody to come between yourself and your particular bully.' Here he extended his arms and emitted a blood-curdling whoop that made the hairs stand on Jonathan Cape's head. He looked around for an avenue of escape, convinced that the middle-aged man before him was about to dismember several members of the class. Instead Roger Wonsit seized the imaginary bully by the hair of the head and swung him round and round as though he were a wet dishcloth.

'When your bully comes into view,' he shouted at the top of his voice, 'what must you do?' The class waited eagerly for the great boxer to continue but Roger was not continuing. He was once more applying his tried and trusted psychology of allowing his words to sink in. After several moments he clapped his hands together and asked for the second time: 'What must you do when your bully stands before you?'

When no answer came, as expected, he provided one.

'You must go for his jugular. Forget the size of him and the weight of him. Just go for him and get stuck in. Now what do you do when you see your bully?' The class responded at once, even Jonathan Cape.

'You must go for his jugular and get stuck in.'

'Again.' Roger Wonsit lifted his outstretched palms demanding a more forceful response. This time the class went overboard as such classes do when given the slightest opportunity. Satisfied that he could elicit no more by way of vocal reply he executed a neat dance around the room, shadow boxing and flooring imaginary assailants at every hand's turn. If asked, most of the boys' parents would be hard put to recall the championship bouts won by Roger Wonsit. They would remember him as an amateur boxer all right and they would remember that he was without peer when it came to weaving and to footwork and to wild swings, any one of which would have dispatched his opponent to Kingdom Come had it landed but they could not recall any knock-outs. The boys' teacher would agree but a number of the more gullible females in the parish had insisted that Roger be allowed talk to the boys.

The emergence, after a long period of relative peace, of several youthful bullies, had prompted the action in the first place. The school-teacher first approached his headmaster, an elderly chap justly famed for his sarcastic comments, and asked for his approval.

'Who did you say?' the headmaster asked in disbelief.

'Roger Wonsit,' his assistant informed him.

'Roger Wonsit,' said the headmaster wearily as was his way, 'would not beat a dead dog. In fact,' he continued, 'Roger Wonsit would not beat the snow off his own overcoat.'

Having rid himself of his daily spew of sarcasm he confided to his assistant that he had no objection to the proposal.

On his way home Jonathan Cape dawdled as only schoolboys dawdle and have been dawdling since the first school was established. As he gazed through a confectioner's window he was joined by his friend Bob's Bobby, an unkempt lad with tousled hair and a wide gap in his upper teeth.

Bob's Bobby was of the travelling people. Confined now to the town's suburbs because of the severity of the winter they would stay put till spring came over the window sill as the song says. Then they would move into the countryside and Bob's Bobby's schooling would end temporarily and prematurely as it did every year.

Like most of his kind Bob's Bobby had little interest in

schooling. The teacher understood his feelings in this respect and left him alone for the most part provided he behaved himself.

Jonathan Cape counted the meagre coins which he had withdrawn from his pocket.

'Come on!' he elbowed his friend and made his way into the confectioner's where he went directly to a blonde-haired, rather corpulent young woman who greeted him by his first name.

'A currant bun if you please Miss Polly.' Jonathan handed over the coins and if Miss Polly noticed that there was a minor deficit she kept it to herself and rung up the amount received on the till behind her back.

Outside the shop the boys stood silently examining the bun which sat invitingly on Jonathan's palm. With a skill beyond his years Jonathan managed to divide the bun into two fair halves. He handed one to his friend and if you think that they gobbled the halves down at once then you don't know boys. They consumed the delicate pastry crumb by crumb as only small boys can and when they finished they licked their fingers clean and they ran their tongues around their mouths lest a solitary particle escape. This is not to say that small boys do not wolf and gobble. Of course they do but there are times when the fare is scarce and it is at these times that they prolong the consumption of the delicacy although it must be said that they are not above retaining choice pieces for the very end and these they may well gobble like starving wolves. It is the way of all boys and many adults.

On their way homeward they spoke of many things and then there came the subject of bullies. They were agreed that bullies were best avoided and neither would subscribe to the way-out views of Roger Wonsit. His name, Bob's Bobby recalled, had often come up at night as the travelling folk sat around their campfire. It was Bob's Bobby's grandfather Big Bob who had mentioned the boxer's name.

'I saw him fight once,' the old man told the extended family as they savoured the heat from the glowing logfire. 'In those days he was called Killer Wonsit but I shall never know why for as far as I could see, he was not possessed of the power to kill a butterfly. On the night I saw him he was fighting a man called Crusher Kaly and I shall never know why for he would not crush a skinless banana. They fought for three rounds and not a single blow was struck although I must admit that both boxers left the ring hardly able to stand. I remember they made a lot of noises and they threw a lot of punches but they hadn't a scratch between them when the final bell sounded. The two together would not make one fighting man.'

The young friends parted at Jonathan Cape's front door. Sometimes Jonathan would accompany Bob's Bobby to the campsite and already Jonathan was well acquainted with Big Bob and other lesser-known members of the travelling clan. However, on this particular occasion, Jonathan made the excuse that he had errands to run. He did not say that the real reason was fear of meeting a bully. Truth to tell there was only one real bully in the community and he was newly-emerged. He had not yet attracted any henchmen although there was one small, harmless boy who followed him about wherever he went. Already the bully whose sobriquet happened to be Pugface had beaten up several younger bullies and was in receipt of weekly dividends from a score or so of terrified small boys in whom he had successfully invested his time and intimidatory tactics. He didn't have to beat up these victims of his terror campaign. The fame of Pugface had spread throughout the town but only among the schoolchildren. It was their secret and even their parents were in the dark as to the identity of the wretch who was responsible for the sleepless, tortured nights of their offspring.

Pugface had threatened his victims with absolute dismemberment should they breathe a word of his existence to anybody.

Imagine the horror experienced by Jonathan Cape when there was no response to his frenzied knocking just as Pugface, trailed by his satellite, came swaggering down the street. Jonathan's mother, if only he had known, was next door copying a yuletide recipe from her neighbour. Jonathan tried to make himself look smaller as Pugface drew near but failed utterly in his first attempt at self-diminishment.

'Got any money boy?' The question came from the uncouth, over-grown twelve year-old who stood towering above him.

If only I hadn't purchased that bun, Jonathan Cape thought.

'You deaf boy?' The second question was accompanied by a vicious wigging of Jonathan's left ear. When the bully let go Jonathan remembered Roger Wonsit's words. He withdrew several yards to the bigger boy's astonishment.

'Go for the jugular!' That's what Wonsit had said. Jonathan did not know exactly where the jugular was situated but he suspected it must be somewhere downstairs or else he would surely have heard his mother use it. He bent his head and ran at his tormentor with a high-pitched squeal. Almost at once, after he had rebounded, he found himself on the flat of his back. Pugface lifted him to his feet by the hair of his head.

'You have my money ready for me next time we meet, you hear boy, else you won't reckernise yourself when you look in the mirror.'

'Sure!' Jonathan assured him.

'You won't forget boy!' Pugface was now wigging the right ear.

'I won't! I won't! I won't!' Jonathan promised. Later he might have told his mother or he might have told his father who had been a crack footballer in his heyday but a fitful sleep full of nightmares would pass before he confided in anybody. After school he informed his friend Bob's Bobby of the previous afternoon's disaster. Christmas was but three days distant and if Jonathan was to hand over his Christmas money there would be nothing left for presents. The friends decided that under no circumstances should any money be handed over. Bob's Bobby was emphatic especially since Jonathan had disclosed to him some weeks before that he intended buying him a Christmas present.

'And I'll get you one too,' Bob's Bobby had replied although after this impetuous promise he did not know where the money for such a luxury would come from. The travellers had little money and the little they had they needed for food and clothing and sometimes for medicine and professional treatment for their sick horses and ponies.

After school the friends decided on a circuitous way home. Bob's Bobby went first so that Jonathan would have time to beat a hasty retreat should his tormentor appear.

'He won't bother with me,' Bob's Bobby explained. 'I don't have any money and I don't have nowhere to get money.' Having escorted his charge to his front door and having waited till he was safely indoors Bob's Bobby hurried homewards, not because he was afraid of Pugface but because he wished to consult his grandfather before the old man departed to the next county where he planned to spend the twelve days of Christmas with his youngest daughter who happened to be married to a travelling man with a loose base in that part of the world. Bob's Bobby found the old man about to depart. First he asked him about the likely locations of red-berried holly trees and then he told him of Jonathan Cape's predicament. Small bearts* of red-berried holly sold at one shilling each and there was, Bob's Bobby reckoned, enough time left to him before Christmas to dispose of sufficient bearts to meet his financial requirements for Christmas.

The old man disclosed the whereabouts of three giant holly trees in the extreme corner of a distant wood.

'Cut your branches cleanly and then only the tiniest,' the old traveller warned. 'This way the trees will not suffer and other branches will grow in place of those you cut. For God's sake do not hack or bend or pull branches or the trees will suffer great pain.'

Bob's Bobby promised Big Bob that the trees would not be injured.

'Now,' said his grandfather, 'what was this other matter

* *Bundles*

you wanted to talk about?' Briefly Bob's Bobby ran though the events of the day and the day before.

'I know him to see him,' Big Bob informed his grandson, 'and he's no different from any other bully except that this fellow is blubber from head to toe and will not last long in a scrap. Still he's big and blustery and by now he's used to scaring people so he thinks he's tough.' Followed by his grandson, Big Bob led the way to a small alder grove out of earshot of the makeshift canvas tents and other improvised shelters. There were caravans too, brightly painted down to the very wheelspokes, canvas-covered as well and not at all unlike the covered wagons used by the early American trail-blazers as they pioneered their way across an undeveloped continent.

'This Pugface,' Big Bob lit his pipe and allowed the blue smoke to ascend through the branches overhead, 'will fall or maybe run the same as all his kind as soon as he meets anybody who'll stand up to him. As far as I can see your friend Jonathan Cape is not this person although from what you've told me he does not seem wanting in courage. Courage alone is never enough when you're dealing with somebody twice your size so it seems to me that you are the very man to deal with Pugface.'

'Me!' Bob's Bobby could scarcely restrain the laughter which came surging from his throat. Ignoring the outburst his grandfather led him by the hand through the grove until they reached an ancient stile which led into an even more ancient graveyard.

'Your great-grandfather, who was my father, lies over there where the ivy climbs the wall near the corner. He was the smallest of all his brothers and some say he was the smallest traveller that ever lived in this part of the country. Yet, for all that, he beat four well-known bullies in the same day in four different places and at the end of that day they stopped being bullies for the rest of their lives. In many ways you resemble him. You have his eyes and you have his hair but now you must ask yourself if you have his wiles and above all you must ask yourself if you have his heart so what you must do is go over to his grave and ask him for the loan of his wiles and the loan of his heart. If a voice comes up out of the ground that says no it will mean that he doesn't want you to have them but if there is no answer by the count of three sevens it will mean that he has passed the things you need over to you. So long as you have his heart and his wiles you need fear no man. Off with you now and I will stand here till you return.'

Big Bob smiled grimly as he watched his nimble grandson leap from mound to mound towards the grave and at the same time, as his grandfather's smile grew grimmer, to his first brush with those who would deny him and deny his friends their natural rights. He watched as the skinny figure made the sign of the cross and he laughed aloud when, at the end of his supplication, he leaped into the air a transformed person. He arrived breathless at Big Bob's side.

'You feel better now?' his grandfather asked.

Bob's Bobby nodded.

'And you feel bigger now?'

'Oh yes. Much bigger,' came the reply.

'All you have to do now is walk up to Pugface in the schoolyard tomorrow and invite him to fight.' Big Bob made it sound as if it was a run-of-the-mill task. His grandson nodded eagerly.

'Now let us return to the camp and on our way I will tell you a few things which will make your job easier. Naturally you will keep these things to yourself or you'll lose your advantage before you begin.'

'Naturally,' came back the positive response. That night the newly-infused champion of civil liberties slept soundly and did not awaken until his mother called him for school. His breakfast consisted of a pannyfull of sweetened oatmeal porridge and he devoured it with a relish.

As usual during the lunch break the schoolyard was crowded. Pugface stood in the centre surrounded by his fear-filled followers. Bob's Bobby swung him around sharply and invited him to fight after school at a particular place where schoolboys had fought for generations. The venue was an ancient, tree-lined lane which led to the river bank. Mostly the place was deserted although when darkness fell courting couples would converge on the area, sometimes reclining in amorous embraces against the trunks of the giant beeches and, other times, when the moon was visible, walking the river bank hand in hand.

Pugface was temporarily at a loss for words and while he futilely instituted a search for same a crowd of schoolboys began to gather. All eyes were focused on Pugface. Bob's Bobby stood with his skinny legs apart awaiting an answer, his great-grandfather's burning eyes fixed unwaveringly on those of the school's most notorious bully, still speechless and under mounting pressure to make a statement.

The laughter which should have surfaced at the tiny traveller's outrageous challenge was stifled by the intensity of his glare and by the rigidity of his stance.

Only a few moments before a rumour had spread like wildfire through the playground. Bob's Bobby, for all his insignificance and despite his tender years, had killed a grown man with a single kidney punch, a Tasmanian backhander, during a summer altercation at the great fair of Puck in Killorglin in the county of Kerry. It was certain that nobody in the school, the teachers apart, knew the precise whereabouts of the kidneys and it was even more certain that nobody, the teachers included, would ever before have heard of a Tasmanian backhander and how would they when the now oft-repeated phrase had, until that time, belonged exclusively to the vocabulary of Big Bob the traveller who had created it only the day before.

The story of the Killorglin massacre, started initially by Jonathan Cape, had now spread to every corner of the school ground and still, after all this time, Pugface had not responded to Bob's Bobby's challenge nor had he even decided whether he should take the challenge seriously. Finally he spoke.

'After school,' he growled, 'I'll kill you stone dead. First I'll tear off your ears and I'll keep them for my cat. Then I'll tear out your heart and I'll keep it for my dog. Then I'll break your legs and your hands and your head.'

'After school.' Bob's Bobby joined his friend Jonathan Cape who stood near the front of the onlooking throng. The pair decided to return earlier than usual to their classroom. 'We will take this puffed sciortán* from your withers,' Bob's

*A leech

Bobby assured his friend, 'and that will be my Christmas present to you.'

It was his grandfather who had made the original statement regarding the sciortán, his final words, before his departure for his daughter's home in west Cork.

Through the branches of the great trees the sun's rays shed a mottled light on the riverside arena where two hundred schoolboys had gathered to witness the demolition of Bob's Bobby. They were not quite convinced that he had killed a man at the fair of Killorglin and, even if he had, it was certain that members of his clan were at hand to render assistance but every schoolboy would agree that the travelling folk were wily and fearless and there was no doubt about the fact that they would have a variety of ploys and stratagems to suit every occasion. They were most eager to witness, for the first time, the execution of the Tasmanian backhander. Some were sceptical but the majority would have seen the fighting men of the travellers in action at fairs and festivals where they would resort to the most outlandish stratagems in order to gain the upper hand.

'Right, make a ring!' The curt command came from a senior boy whose father was a teacher in the school. It was apparent that some of the father's authority had rubbed off on the son for a ring was created almost immediately and a great hush ensued while the self-appointed master of ceremonies raised his hands aloft and called upon the protagonists to enter the circle. First in was Pugface, shadow-boxing as he entered and snorting like a regular professional as he delivered deadly blows from every angle. The onlookers screamed and shouted at the tops of their yet unbroken voices. Bob's

Bobby's entry was less dramatic than his rival's. His approach was indifferent and even reposeful especially when his supporters, and they were in a majority, cheered him until their lungs were fit to burst.

The master of ceremonies now took up his position between the opponents.

'Is it to be a fight to the finish?' he demanded in stentorian tones.

'Yes. Yes!' two hundred voices answered frenetically before either of the principals had a chance to approve or disapprove.

'I'll count to ten,' the master of ceremonies spoke shrilly, 'and when the count is concluded the fight will begin and it will be a fight to the finish.'

He pushed the waiting pugilists well apart but before he could commence the count Bob's Bobby took off his tattered shortcoat and folded it neatly before handing it to his second who chanced to be none other than Jonathan Cape. He then spat on his hands while the onlookers remarked that they had never in their lives beheld such a look in any man's eyes before. The burning orbs fixed themselves on those of Pugface who bent his head unable to withstand the baleful glare of the tiny traveller. The taking off of the shortcoat had unnerved him. Worse was to follow.

Spitting on his hands a second time Bob's Bobby took off his frayed shirt and folded it neatly. Again he handed it over to his second. The wily traveller then removed his vest until he stood bare from the waist up. He flexed his wrists as an excited murmur ran through the crowd. Could this be the prelude to the devastating Tasmanian backhander? They were never to find out for Pugface's courage, already wilting after the divesting of the shortcoat, went into sharper decline after the taking off of the shirt. A cold fear gripped him when the last garment of the upper body was handed over to a grinning Jonathan Cape. Why was Cape grinning? Why was the traveller so cocksure? Why did his own hands shake and why did his knees weaken? Why did he wish he was somewhere else all of a sudden and why did the traveller's eyes burn like glowing embers so that his own eyes were blinded and he was unable to see straight? With a cry of indescribable passion the young traveller sunk his teeth into the side of his lower lip. The red blood spurted forth and ran down his chin, coursed down his neck and spread itself over his chest. With a second even more unnerving shriek he rubbed the blood all over his face and arms. Several faint-hearted onlookers took flight. Others, unaccustomed to the sight of blood, fell insensible to the ground.

Bob's Bobby now presented an absolutely hideous sight. The blood drained from the drooling visage of his disintegrating opponent and, worst of all, the shrieking, demoniacal, blood-covered impish traveller was about to launch his first attack. Pugface staggered backwards uttering strange sounds made up of gasps and whimpers and sobs. Then suddenly he turned and ran for his life pursued by Bob's Bobby and Jonathan Cape and a score of other victims of his vile intimidation. They followed him through the streets of the astonished town until he arrived at his own door, a wretched figure still slobbering and sobbing. He disappeared indoors without a single, solitary look behind and was not seen in public for a full week. When he reappeared he was a different Pugface, kind, thoughtful, considerate and courteous to young and old.

He would so remain for the remainder of his natural life and when he died prematurely trying to save a drowning cat his was one of the largest funerals ever seen in the district. The travelling folk said of him that he went straight to heaven and that he was embraced three times by Saint Peter at the pearly gates. After the fight Bob's Bobby, accompanied by his faithful friend, returned to the grave of his great-grandfather where he ceremoniously returned the wiles and the heart he had borrowed. He would never seek a loan of them again for to have these precious things once, even for a short while, is to have them forever. The Christmas that followed was the best for many a year especially for small boys.

CHRISTMAS NOSES

THERE ARE MORE NOSES BLOWN AT CHRISTMAS than any other time of year and, believe me, noses need blowing just as their proprietors need Christmas.

Let me put it another way gentle reader. We don't blow our noses just to clear them or to make loud or rude noises.

There are many hard-faced gents abroad, especially during Christmas, with soft hearts. These unfortunates are slow to express their feelings until they have a certain amount of intoxicating drink aboard. Even then they are reluctant to express their more profound emotions.

What they do instead is to produce large handkerchiefs into which they blow their real feelings. One has to listen closely. Nothing more is required. The baying and the snorting and the trumpeting to which the listener's ears are subjected can be interpreted as expressions of love and concern as fond and as genuine as any which escape all too rarely from the confines of the human heart. How's that William Wordsworth puts it:

> Thanks for the human heart by which we live
> Thanks for its tenderness, its joys, its fears.
> To me the meanest flower that grows can give
> Thoughts that do often lie too deep for tears.

Nose-blowing becomes the elderly more than the young and this may well be because elderly noses are larger and veinier and hairier and pucer. Give me an old nose any day of the week before a young nose. There are no reverberations when young noses are blown. In fact you have to tell young folk that they should blow their noses. Old folk blow like nobody's business which is good for noses and old folk alike.

Then there are certain young gentlemen who blow their noses when there is no need whatsoever to do so. They believe that it matures them. They remind me, in many respects, of those young men who sport moustaches and even beards which they hope will make them look older.

These undeveloped nose-blowings have a false ring to them. They are hollow-sounding. They are easily identified by the experienced ear or by anybody whose parents or grand-parents were nose-blowers. I could always distinguish my father's nose-blowing from other nose-blows and whenever I heard him in the distance I was instantly reassured that all was well with the world.

Then there are gents who blow their noses in order to make themselves look more manly but it never comes off. The sounds are like those made by baby elephants who have become separated from their mothers whereas the genuine article, the full male outpouring from the facial proboscis, has all the powerful vibrancy of a rogue elephant.

I recall too when I was a boy there were severe-faced old gents of irascible dispositions who would blow their noses at people to intimidate them. It worked in most cases but never when the nose was blown at another nose-blower.

A nose blown properly and from the correct angle often

put a man on the right road just as surely as a kick on the posterior did. In order to realise maximum effect, however, the nose should be blown in quiet or hallowed places where silence dominates. A nose suddenly blown at full force in a silent room can send a surprised assailant scuttling for shelter.

There is only one occasion when I find nose-blowing to be extremely shattering and that is when I am the proprietor of a hangover. I always run for my life when I see a nose-blower approaching. Let him blow by all means as long as I am out of range.

On the credit side I heard of a nose-blower in a distant land who once blew a hole in his handkerchief when his prodigal son came home and another who blew off his own hat when he sneezed on Christmas Eve after his grand-daughter had told him she loved him.

I am of the belief that no house should be without a nose-blower. A good, snorting, rattling, bellicose nose-blow will frighten away intruders far better than a barking dog. The criminal will always know that a bark came from a dog but with a comprehensive nose-blow who is to say that the blower is not a polar bear or a tiger or even an elephant!

However, it must be finally said that a good nose-blow into a voluminous handkerchief is the last refuge of the inarticulate, especially those shy souls, who long to tell of their love and concern during the glowing days of Christmas.

HIGH
FIELDING

JACK FROST WASN'T AS COLD OR AS pinched as his name might suggest. No, he was bluff and hale and hearty, always ostentatiously and good naturedly slapping down a large denomination note on the collection tables which were strategically placed Sunday after Sunday around the entrance to the church on behalf of some charity or other. Yet Jack wasn't popular. He wasn't half as well-liked, for instance, as Dinny Doublesay who contributed very little to charities for the good reason that he didn't have an awful lot to give. Of course, Dinny had played football with the local team when he was in his heyday and he had a way with the girls or so they said. Also he was trainer-in-chief of the highly successful under-14 team year in, year out, so that he was highly regarded by parents and youngsters alike. Jack Frost did not like Dinny Doublesay. He once confided to his wife that he hated the sight of him although when pressed for a reason he couldn't say why.

'Could it be,' she asked, 'because everybody else likes him?'

'It could be,' Jack replied peevishly, 'and it could also be something else like he's lousy and warty and picks his nose and he's always chasing after women.'

'But he's a widower,' his wife argued, 'and there's no restriction on widowers.'

'Shut up,' Jack Frost shouted at her and he drew the bedclothes over his head. Jack's wife laughed herself gently to sleep wondering how it was that there had never been an open confrontation between her husband and the man he despised. Certainly the town was small enough and how often did they drink in Gilhaffy's, the football pub where the game's players and aficionados gathered after every championship encounter!

She knew that Jack often tended to bide his time, always on the lookout for an opportunity to get even with somebody who had taken him down or with somebody he didn't like for reasons that he couldn't altogether explain.

She knew Jack Frost. She had been married to him and to the business for thirty years. Jack was sly for all his apparent heartiness and in business there was nobody as devious. He overcharged whenever he thought he would get away with it and as for giving proper weight and measure, well! All Jack's instincts would be opposed to such a dictum. Once when he had overcharged an elderly female for poor quality sausages his wife had taken him aside and told him firmly that it was wrong.

'Of course it is,' Jack agreed, 'but it's also wrong for her to hide boxes of sardines in her cleavage every time she thinks nobody's looking and it's wrong for her to keep popping grapes into her mouth when she has no notion of buying any.'

The confrontation which Kate Frost had long anticipated and dreaded took place one late evening at the meat counter in the supermarket. Jack was, as usual, immaculately dressed in freshly-laundered white coat and cap and greeted each and every customer as though they were long-lost relatives who had been sorely missed. His smile disappeared when he beheld Dinny Doublesay even though the latter had a twenty pound note in his hand. Jack Frost accepted the note with a curt thank you after he had wrapped and handed Dinny the four slices of lamb's liver for which he had declared a preference over chops, steaks and kidneys.

Jack placed the note in the till and then sweetly, smilingly and mischievously handed his victim the change out of a ten pound note.

'I gave you twenty,' Dinny Doublesay spoke matter-of-factly not wishing to draw attention to himself.

'You're sure it wasn't a hundred you gave me!' Jack Frost threw out the question for the benefit of everybody within earshot. Dinny Doublesay pursed his lips and availed of the silence which had imposed itself with deadly impact all round.

'I gave you twenty,' he spoke evenly, 'and you gave me the change out of ten which means you've taken me down for ten pounds.'

'Why don't you come in here and have a look at the contents of the till and then we'll see who's codding who?'

Jack Frost stood to one side in order to allow access to his accuser. A number of shoppers surged forward lest they miss the outcome. As the till drawers shot forward Dinny moved in to investigate but was forestalled by Jack Frost.

'Let's have a pair of independent witnesses.' The supermarket proprietor raised a hand and intimated to a pair of females that they should come forward and authenticate the outcome.

Dinny Doublesay in their presence instituted a fruitless search which would be repeated over and over, at Jack Frost's urgings, by the pair of female witnesses who would declare that there was no twenty pound note to be seen. There were numerous five and ten pound notes but not a solitary twenty.

'Satisfied Mr Doublesay!' Jack Frost slammed the till shut and devoted his attention to the pair who had vindicated him. Dinny stood irresolutely to one side before shuffling his way towards the main exit. He was confused and embarrassed. He could have sworn that he had a twenty pound note in his hand and that he handed it to Jack Frost. He decided to go home. His daughter would know for sure. Had she not handed him the money as he left the house!

In his wake Jack Frost was escorting the two witnesses to the wine shelves where they would choose one of the more expensive vintages in return for their honesty and integrity.

'Witnesses' expenses!' Jack had laughed aloud as he beamed on all and sundry. Word of the incident would later spread but nobody believed, the witnesses apart, that Jack Frost was innocent. There were many who would recall similar experiences. When he reached home Dinny Doublesay sat on his favourite chair. His daughter, sensing that something was seriously amiss, sat on hers.

'Did you or did you not give me a twenty pound note when I left the house awhile back?' Dinny asked.

'I gave you a twenty pound note,' his daughter informed him.

Later in the back room at Gilhaffy's Dinny Doublesay's many friends in the footballing world commiserated with him, three of his closer cronies in particular. These would be the

Maglane brothers Johnny, Jerry and Jimmy who once formed the nucleus of the local football team. They played at left half forward, centre forward and right half forward respectively and when they combined as a unit there was no holding them. They specialised particularly in long passes by hand or foot which often saw the ball travel over distances of forty yards where one of the trio would have surreptitiously removed himself so that he would be in a position to gather the pass and send it over or under the bar for a vital score.

They were, according to local newspaper reporters, imaginative, innovative, accurate and mercurial but it was their passing from improbable distances that set them apart.

Often in the back room at Gilhaffy's followers of the code would ask each other to nominate the best player that ever togged out for the team and invariably the answer would come back – 'I don't know who the best player was but I know who the best three players were.'

The Maglanes were particularly close to Dinny Doublesay. Dinny was the team's full forward when the Maglanes were in the ascendancy. They put many a score his way, unselfishly passing from less favourable distances to where Dinny was disposed near the edge of the square.

'Combine!' Johnny Maglane was fond of saying before championship finals. 'Combine and nothing will beat us!'

'Submerge yourselves!' Jerry Maglane would counsel, 'and rise as one so that we will form an unstoppable wave.' Jerry was the poet of the Maglane family and in fact had composed several ballads about the exploits and triumphs of the team.

'A team that doesn't play together won't stay together,'

Jimmy Maglane would say as the fifteen players primed each other before running on to the field fired with resolve and gleaming with embrocation.

Uppermost in the thoughts of all those congregated in the back room at Gilhaffy's was how to get even with Jack Frost. Violence was outlawed since the team's greatest successes were achieved in the face of violence by the expedient of not reacting and by playing the game according to the rules.

As well as being poetic Jerry Maglane was also the strategist of the team. It was he who laid out the plan of play and it was he who might suddenly order a change of tactics which often turned defeat into victory. There is no element of humanity as potent or as loyal or as dangerous or as compassionate towards each other as the survivors of a once-successful football team. There is that quiet confidence in themselves. There is the certain knowledge that when they present a united front they can achieve anything. That is why none interfered with Jerry Maglane as he figured out a way to get even with Jack Frost.

He sat, isolated, humming and hawing to himself, scratching his nose, his forehead and his jaw in turn. He pulled upon his ear lobes as though they were the handles of pumps which would send mighty ideas gushing to his brain. From time to time they surveyed him anxiously.

'Ah yes!' he announced triumphantly at the end of his deliberations, 'I see it all now.'

Johnny Maglane placed a pint of stout in his brother's hand. Nobody knew better than he of the strain to which Jerry had been subjected while he deliberated. None would ask him to reveal his plan. All would be known in due course and this made the prospect of restitution all the sweeter.

Later when the lights had been dimmed in the back room and only the nucleus of the town's best-ever team remained, Jerry Maglane told of his requirements.

'I will need,' said he, 'our two best fielders and our best long passer. No more will I say till the deed is done and our comrade's honour is avenged.'

Here he laid a hand on the shoulder of Dinny Doublesay as a tear moistened his eye and the lips that issued many a stern command on the playing field trembled with emotion.

'All I will say to you,' he addressed himself to the former full forward, 'is that under no circumstances are you to buy a solitary item for Christmas nor are you to utter a solitary word to any man or woman until our business is done.'

The nights passed slowly thereafter and as they did the Christmas fever mounted until its spirit was everywhere abroad. Two nights before the blessed event there was an extension of shopping hours until nine o'clock.

Shortly before the extension ended Johnny Maglane and his wife Pidge arrived at Jack Frost's supermarket ostensibly to purchase some groceries to tide them over the Christmas holiday.

'I want you,' Johnny Maglane informed Pidge, 'to engage Jack Frost in conversation. Make sure that his back is turned to me at all times.'

Pidge Maglane nodded eagerly. She was well aware that there was something afoot and she was only too eager to be part of it. Dinny Doublesay ranked high among her friends and she was as anxious as the other conspirators to see the score settled. Also she had no doubt about her ability to engage and absorb Jack Frost in a long and interesting conversation. Jack, for his part, had often cast a longing eye in the direction of the footballer's wife.

'Dang it!' he often whispered to himself, 'I will never understand how those danged footballers with nothing in their heads wind up with such good-looking women. I mean,' he would continue to confide to himself, 'what have they got that I haven't got and yet the best of women fall for these so-called athletes who, more often than not, kick the danged ball wide.'

It was a question that he would never successfully answer. When Pidge Maglane approached him and suggested they remove themselves to a quiet area he jumped at the opportunity and when they arrived at a secluded spot behind the dog-and-cat foot pyramids he waited eagerly for some heart-lifting revelation. For awhile she did not speak for the good reason that she could think of nothing to say.

'Well!' Jack Frost moved from one foot to the other.

'Well!' Pidge Maglane echoed the question as she racked her brains for something to say.

'Oh yes,' she said in a confidential tone as though what she was about to say had slipped her mind and had suddenly presented itself again.

'I was wondering,' Pidge Maglane opened, 'if you would consider joining our drama society?'

Jack Frost was astonished.

'Me!' was all he could say.

'I don't see why not,' Pidge Maglane was in full flight now. 'I mean you have the appearance and you have the carriage. Carriage is ninety percent of acting. Then you're sharp. I mean you wouldn't have any trouble remembering lines. I'm sure you know the price of everything on those shelves and if you can memorise such prosaic things as prices you can memorise anything. Then there's your voice. It's so seductive and yet so resonant. Then there are your eyes, those come-to-bed eyes. Man dear you were born for the stage!'

It was at this stage of the conversation that the object whizzed by over-head.

'What was that?' Jack Frost asked, looking up anxiously but seeing nothing.

'What was what?' Pidge Maglane asked although fully aware that something had passed by in the space above them.

'Never mind, never mind!' Jack Frost dismissed the intrusion and wished only for his unexpected veneration to continue. It was, in fact, a ten pound trussed turkey enshrouded in plastic wrapping which had passed. It had been thrown by Pidge's husband Johnny who had lifted it from a display case and, when he was certain nobody was looking, flung it a full forty yards out through the main exit where it was beautifully fielded by his brother Jerry who passed it at least fifty more yards to the third Maglane brother Jimmy who fielded it with great skill before placing it in the open booth of his car. There followed a ham, cooked and wrapped and if the Maglane brothers had fielded well in their respective heydays they fielded magnificently now but the skills of Jerry and Jimmy were shortly to be put to an unprecedented test by the oldest brother who, for good measure, had lifted a bottle of Cuvée Dom Perignon 1985 from the wine shelf, had lovingly handled it feeling its weight and balance and dispatched it faithfully and accurately into the waiting hands of the much-lauded fielder, his brother Jerry who flung it in turn to the third brother Jimmy who placed it beside the turkey and ham in the car booth.

After the champagne had been flung Johnny Maglane decided that enough was enough. The three items which had flown through the air with the greatest of ease would more than compensate Dinny Doublesay and by the time the story leaked and reached the ears of Jack Frost, the ham and the turkey would have been devoured. Christmas would have been toasted and the champagne swallowed by Dinny Doublesay and his darling daughter.

A CHRISTMAS DIVERSION

AT SEVENTY-ONE THE BADGER MACMEW RETAINED MOST of the brown, grey-streaked hair which had earned him his soubriquet. Otherwise he didn't look in the least like a badger. He was tall, slender, elegant and courteous which was more than could be said for some of the mischievous neighbours who privately compared him to the carnivorous mammal after which he was named.

'It isn't fair,' Mary Agge Lehone was fond of telling the few elderly customers who still frequented her tiny green-grocery near the end of the long street which had seen better days.

'I mean,' Mary Agge would go on, 'he's so refined and he never badgers anybody. He brings me bags of kindling all the time and he never charges anything. It's all out of the goodness of his heart.'

Part of what Mary Agge said was true. The Badger Mac-Mew, particularly during the long winters, would scour the nearby woodlands for the kindling with which the bright turf fires of the neighbourhood were started.

Though never full, the rickety turf shed at the rear of the Lehone premises was never without a horse-rail or two of turf, not top-quality black turf but sods of brown and grey which burned all too quickly. Black, bottom-sod turf on the other hand, lasted from one end of the day to the other provided, of course, the fire was properly constructed in the first place.

The Badger's turf shed, several doors downwards from Mary Agge's, contained no turf at all. There was some timber and a modest heap of bruscar.* Since the Badger lived off his old-age pension he could not afford to supplement his wood stocks with turf or coal. By careful management and skilful disposition of his bruscar his hearth was never without a small fire while he was indoors. Electricity was still waiting in the wings in those distant days so that it was to native timber and turf that the street's inhabitants turned to keep out the cold and boil the water and cook the food and wash the clothes and the faces and the hands and the bodies and so forth and so on.

Before we proceed further it must be said that it wasn't altogether out of the goodness of his heart that the Badger Mac-Mew saw to the kindling wants of Mary Agge Lehone. The Badger had, all his life, shown a preference for the single state. Mary Agge's late husband Walter had expired suddenly some thirty years before while cleaning the family chimney. The exertions had proved too much for him and when he fell silently to the ground he was already dead. Mary Agge had been thirty-seven at the time and while she might have married during the intervening years she declined many a substantial offer for she was dainty, petite and some said good-looking in her own way. She also had her own home, fronted by the small

* *Kindling*

green-grocery. She knew how to cook and even her detractors would be forced to admit that she never put a hard word on anybody. She received the blessed sacrament every morning of the week and was one of the four select female trios who decorated the altars of the parish church, unfailingly, when it was their turn to do so.

The Badger MacMew, on the other hand, missed mass on occasion and received the sacred host but yearly. He was, however, it was agreed by most, not a bad chap at all and might well see heaven if he mended his ways ever so slightly. He suffered occasionally from severe twinges of arthritis but was otherwise healthy and mobile. He had been a trousers-maker until his sixty-eighth year when his arthritic fingers began to fail him and he was forced into retirement.

When Mary Agge's husband Walter died many felt that she would succumb to grief and die of a broken heart but surprisingly she rallied as most widows do and proceeded to live out her lonely days as content as any woman could be in such a situation. The Badger decided shortly after Walter's burial that he would contribute in his own small way to Mary Agge's upkeep. She would never be without kindling while he could visit the woodlands. Gradually he found himself falling in love with her but he resolved that she must never know. For one thing it might damage their friendship such as it was if he ever confessed his true feelings to her. Then there was the danger that she might be so deeply offended that she might sever the relationship permanently. He chose to keep his mouth shut and pray that she might deduce from the quality and consistency of the kindlings that he cherished her above all others and would do so till his last lopping crumbled silently into the ashes of her hearth. He dreamed of her last thing at night and first thing in the morning. He always maintained to himself that it was a small thing which would acquaint her fully of his love for her, some as yet unimagined occasion which would swing things in his favour, some incident or instrument of fate, some insignificant out-of-the-blue factor from which he might find her securely cradled in his arms, her soft hair brushing his ear lobes and her hazel eyes laughing into his.

In his dreams they travelled widely together, sharing the same tastes, revelling in the wild scenery where they would find themselves at the close of day in the presence of incomparable sunsets.

One would never dream from looking at the Badger Mac-Mew that such romantic thoughts dominated his dreaming but such is the reality of life that we should never be surprised by the romantic aspirations of the most unlikely. All humans aspire through fantasy but nominating oneself for the ultimate honours in a close relationship was an undertaking fraught with hazards. That was the reason the Badger had become a perpetual bidder of time like millions of other no-hopers in every corner of the human world. He was well aware that others in the vicinity were desirous of advancing their causes through fair means or foul in the direction of his beloved Mary Agge. His worst fear was that she might suddenly be swept off her feet by a dark horse in a late surge while he dawdled and hoped for a miracle. In this respect there was one individual he feared more than any other. In his estimation the person in question was a loud-mouthed, scurrilous pervert by the name of Danny Sagru. Every street, he thought bitterly, had its Danny Sagru. He was, therefore, astonished one day to hear the very same scoundrel being described by none other than Mary Agge herself as not a bad oul' fella.

Not a bad oul' fella! He repeated the undeserved delineation to himself several times. Oh dear, oh dear! How naive was womanhood and how gormless was this unfortunate woman in particular!

Danny Sagru was, without doubt, the most unpopular man in the entire street, the entire parish. If you were to scour the highways and byways you would be hard put to find somebody with a good word to say about him. There were a number of reasons for this. He owned most of the land roundabout. He was wealthier than even Tom Shine the draper, Joe Willies the baker, Ned Hobbs the grocer.

Danny Sagru didn't carry his wealth well. He boasted about it. He rattled the silver in his trousers pockets and he regularly flicked the chunky wad of notes which he had no need to carry about with him.

If he ever gave a small boy a penny he would always charge the recipient to inform all and sundry that Danny Sagru had given it to him.

He never subscribed to charities and yet Mary Agge Lehone had publicly stated that he was not a bad oul' fella. He was an oul' fella all right, the Badger would subscribe to this. He was several years older than the Badger although he did not look as if he was. He had an appetite like a horse but wait, the Badger began a reassessment of his arch-rival.

If he was placed under oath the Badger would have to admit that the scoundrel possessed a certain degree of spurious loyalty. He would have to concede that Danny Sagru always purchased his vegetables from Mary Agge Lehone and from Mary Agge Lehone alone. Let the cabbage be wrinkled, the spuds watery, the turnips frostbitten. Let her parsnips be shrivelled, her carrots shrunken, her cauliflowers browning! It mattered not to Danny Sagru and there was another even more worrying aspect of his purchases. He never questioned her prices. There was an extravagance about him as he pressed the coins into the cup of her hand.

'Your change, your change,' she would call after him as he exploded through the shop door, cabbages in one hand, potato satchel in the other.

'Keep it, keep it,' he would call back as though it were a considerable sum, whereas in reality, it never exceeded a halfpenny.

For all his wealth Danny Sagru had never forsaken the modest home where he first saw the light. The house, like all the others including Mary Agge's, was two-storeyed and two-bedroomed with a back shed, always filled to capacity with black, heavy sods. There was access from the shed to a long but narrow backway along which ran the seventy or more backsheds which housed the fuel supplies for the corresponding front or street houses. All looked alike, all with pitch painted corrugated iron roofs, all rickety and in need of restructuring, all save that of Danny Sagru, which was a model of its kind and which was crammed from bottom to top with turf sods as black as the ace of spades, heavy as lead and more lasting than coal.

Danny had several suppliers who were acquainted from long experience with his precise needs. Turf-cutters with horse-drawn, clamped rails of the precious bottom sods, would arrive regularly at the Sagru shed and deposit their loads. There was a fixed rate and seasoned turf-cutters would say to novices 'You don't renege on him and he won't renege on you. You'll get nothing extra but you will get your due.'

Then as happens every ten years or so there came a poor turf harvest. The less well-off suffered most. Danny Sagru suffered not at all. Widows and waifs in the vicinity might perish with the cold but Danny held fast to the sods he had. His poorer neighbours knew that it would be a waste of time to plead for a sod or two to tide them over till the bogs dried so that suppliers might gain access to their turf banks. Like the Badger MacMew they traversed the woodlands near and far for kindling.

The Badger led parties of youngsters to likely places where old logs had lain rotting for years. They sawed and hacked and somehow managed to acquire hearthfuls of fuel to see them through. All the while, through the long nights, Danny Sagru sat in front of his warm fire, occasionally adding to the brightness and redness of his ulcerous nose by the simple expedient of swallowing glass after glass of punch. None shared his hearth, no dog nor cat nor chick nor child nor neighbour nor friend. What he savoured he savoured alone.

Alas for Mary Agge Lehone her fires grew smaller but they never went out. The Badger MacMew saw to that. The Badger MacMew gave all he had until the frost silently laid its cold, white mantle over field and bogland, over street, backway and rooftop. The frost was but a day in residence when Danny Sagru was astonished by the inroads the bad weather had made into his turf. Instead of tackling his spirited pony to the gleaming trap as was his wont when he wished to visit an outlying cattle fair he hired a hackney car to transport him across the fifteen miles of roadway to the village where the fair would be in progress. With Christmas coming up in a few days and fodder in short supply there would be little demand for store cattle. It was a good time to buy and a man with fodder to spare and money to burn like Danny Sagru might profitably expand his existing stock at no great expense. He had done so many times in the past and, indeed, it was from such fortuitous investments that he built most of his fortune. As they drove towards the village Danny's attention was drawn to a moving vehicle which slowly descended a hilly boreen on its way to the main road.

'Pull up! Pull up!' Danny called to his driver. As the roadbound transport reached the cross which would take it to the village where the fair was in progress Danny emerged from the rear of the hired car and raised a hand, indicating that he had a desire to parley. Before him was stalled at the crossroads one of the largest, highest-clamped, heaviest loads of black turf ever to present itself before the greedy, green eyes of Danny Sagru. The load was drawn by a powerful black mare, sixteen hands high and shimmering with muscle from crest to hock, a beautiful animal and worthy transporter of such a perfectly-clamped cargo.

'How much?' Danny Sagru asked.

The turfman, squat and brown, looked over his merchandise as if he had only then noticed it and took stock of the prosperous-looking individual who posed the question regarding the price.

'One pound, two shillings and sixpence,' came the clipped response.

Danny Sagru advanced and circled the mare and rail, feeling individual sods as he proceeded with his inspection.

'If you'll be good enough to move out of the way now, like a good chap,' the turfman flicked his reins, 'I'll be on my way for you see sir I have clients galore waiting in the village.'

'Hold it! Hold it!' Danny Sagru raised an imperious hand and blocked his way. The mare shook her shining harness and raised her shapely head with its sensitive nose and flickering ears.

'I'll give you your money,' Danny announced calmly, 'but you'll have to deliver to my premises in Ballyfurane.'

'Which is seven miles from here and seven miles back and which adds another shilling to the price for this mare will be in sore need of oats by the time we deliver.' The turfman folded his arms.

'I won't quibble with you,' Danny located the money and handed it over.

'You'll give me a luck penny now!' Danny suggested to the turfman who was quick to point out that luck money only came into question when large sums were involved.

'Do you know me?' Danny asked.

'Sure don't the whole world know you,' the turfman declared.

'Ask any person you meet on your way into town and they'll show you where I hang out,' Danny informed him. 'The turf shed is at the rear of the house and 'tisn't bolted nor locked for as quirky and quare as my neighbours are they're too proud to steal. Off with you now and who knows but we'll do business again.'

'Ballyfurane is out of my way,' the turfman announced as he allowed the mare her head, 'but if the money is right I could see myself doing further business with you.'

The village of Ballyfurane consisted of one long main street and two small side streets. The windows of the small shops along the main thoroughfare were decorated with holly and ivy. Some boasted tinsel and fairylights and a few sported home-made cribs representing the nativity.

With Christmas approaching there was an air of mild anticipation. Shoppers were plentiful and business, if not brisk, was reasonably good which was just about as good as anybody could expect in a small place like Ballyfurane.

When the Angelus bell tolled in memory of the Incarnation, as it did every day at twelve noon, Badger MacMew found himself standing at the quietest of the village's four street corners. His hands were thrust deep into his trousers pockets and there was a faraway look on his unshaven face. He was, however, far from despondent. He had, but a bare five minutes before, delivered a bundle of high-quality kindling to Mary Agge Lehone and she had actually allowed her fingers to rest briefly on the back of his hand by way of appreciation. With recollection he concluded that it would be fairer to say her fingers brushed the back of his hand. Still it was a handsome advance on the smiles with which she had previously rewarded him.

As he looked into the distance he beheld for the first time the high-clamped rail of turf drawn by the black mare, guided by a turfman he had never seen before. He withdrew his hands slowly from his pockets and proceeded in a rambling fashion towards the oncoming transport. The Badger was possessed of the natural curiosity of all villagers everywhere except that in his personal case he was a curious fellow by nature and liked to know at all times what was happening in his bailiwick. As he drew near he was surprised when the mare drew to a halt at the behest of the turfman.

'Excuse me sir!' the turfman respectfully addressed himself to the Badger MacMew. 'I am looking for the premises of Danny Sagru.'

The Badger did not answer at once. The proprietor of the sought after premises was safely out of town and would not be back for some time, probably nightfall since he was partial to strong drink whenever he encountered fellow-members of the cattle-jobbing confraternity.

'Follow me,' the Badger turned on his heels and led the way to the by-way at the rear of the main street. He kept a distance of forty yards between himself and the turfman and he walked along the pavements rather than the roadway so that it might be clearly seen that the turfman and he had no connection with each other. Firstly he led the turfman to a laneway at the back of which was a by-way which would take them albeit circuituously to the backway behind the main street where the many lookalike turf sheds stood side by side. The backway was deserted save for a neighbourhood tomcat who sat on the roof of a shed and took no interest in the proceedings beneath him. In the backway the Badger slowed his gait so that the turfman might catch up with him.

'This is the shed,' he indicated the rickety structure at the rear of Mary Agge Lehone's small shop. 'I'll open the door for you and you can heel it in.'

In no time at all the rail was empty and the turfman on his way homewards by an altogether different egress, indicated by the Badger. It was an egress which would lead him to a little-used boreen which would lead him past the village and on to the main route to his hilly abode. Later that evening he and his wife and family would invest the turf money in their Christmas shopping and a happy and holy Christmas would be had by all.

As soon as the turfman had departed the Badger took it upon himself to call upon Mary Agge. A beaming smile was the essence of her greeting as soon as he entered. They stood there without exchange of words or the need for exchange of words.

'You will find,' the Badger said after a short while, 'a little Christmas gift in your shed and I hope it brings you the warmth and comfort you so richly deserve.'

With that he departed and did not appear on the street again until Christmas Eve. It was nightfall as he walked past her door and at first he thought that the sounds he heard as he went by were the chortlings of a dove but no, it was Mary Agge calling his name, gently ever so gently and but barely discernible even though the street was still. When he entered she closed the door behind them and led the way to the small kitchen where a glowing fire spread heat from the hearth.

'You'll have a drop of whiskey,' she said with a smile, 'and so will I,' and so they did and she invited him back the following day for his Christmas dinner and there was no word from Danny Sagru about his missing turf for he was vain in the extreme and would never give it to say that he had been taken down. It would never occur to him, in a score of years, that the Badger had diverted the turf and that Mary Agge Lehone had burned it.

Indeed the Badger and Mary Agge shared all their Christmas dinners thereafter but not as friends or lovers or anything like that but as man and wife and there need be no worries about their living happily ever after because that was exactly what they did.

THE WOMAN WHO HATED CHRISTMAS

POLLY BAUN DID NOT HATE CHRISTMAS AS some of her more un-
charitable neighbours would have people believe. She merely
disliked it. She was once accused by a local drunkard of trying
to call a halt to Christmas. She was on her way out of church
at the time and the drunkard, who celebrated his own form of
mass by criticising the sermon while he leaned against the outside wall of the church, was seen to push her on the back as
she passed the spot where he leaned. As a result Polly Baun
fell forward and was rendered immobile for a week. She told
her husband that she had slipped on a banana skin because he
was a short-tempered chap. However, he found out from another drunkard who frequented the same tavern that Polly
had been pushed. When he confronted her with his findings
she reluctantly conceded that the second drunkard had been
telling the truth.

'You won't do anything rash!' she beseeched him.

'I won't do anything rash,' Shaun Baun promised, 'but
you will have to agree that this man's energies must be directed in another direction. I mean we can't have him pushing

women to the ground because he disagrees with their views. I mean,' he continued in what he believed to be a reasonable tone, 'if this sort of thing is allowed to go on unchecked no woman will be safe.'

'It doesn't worry me in the least,' Polly Baun assured him.

'That may be,' he returned, 'but the fact of the matter is that no woman deserves to be pushed to the ground.'

Polly Baun decided that the time had come to terminate the conversation. It was leading nowhere to begin with and she was afraid she might say something that would infuriate her husband. He flew off the handle easily but generally he would return to his normal state of complacency after a few brief moments.

As Christmas approached, the street shed its everyday look and donned the finery of the season. Polly Baun made one of her few concessions to Christmas by buying a goose. It was a young goose, small but plump and, most importantly, purchased from an accredited goose breeder. It would suit the two of them nicely. There were no children and there would be no Christmas guests and Polly who was of a thrifty disposition judged that there would also be enough for Saint Stephen's Day. She did not need to be thrifty. The hat shop behind which they lived did a tidy business. The tiny kitchen at the rear of the shop served a threefold purpose all told. As well as being a kitchen it was also a dining area and sitting-room. They might have added on but Polly failed to see the need for this. She was content with what she had and she felt that one of the chief problems with the world was that people did not know when they were well off.

'They should be on their knees all day thanking God,' she

would tell her husband when he brought news of malcontents who lived only to whine.

Shaun Baun sought out and isolated his wife's attacker one wet night a week before Christmas. The scoundrel was in the habit of taking a turn around the town before retiring to the pub for the evening. Shaun Baun did not want to take advantage of him while he might be in his cups and besides he wanted him sober enough to fully understand the enormity of his transgressions.

'You sir!' Shaun Baun addressed his victim in a secluded side street, 'are not a gentleman and neither are you any other kind of man. You knocked my wife to the ground and did not bother to go to her assistance.'

'I was drunk,' came back the reply.

'Being drunk is not sufficient justification for pushing a woman to the ground.'

'I was told,' the drunkard's voice was filled with fear, 'that she hates Christmas.'

'That is not sufficient justification either,' Shaun Baun insisted. The drunkard began to back off as Shaun Baun assumed a fighting pose.

'Before I clobber you,' Shaun Baun announced grimly, 'I feel obliged to correct a mistaken impression you have. My wife does not hate Christmas as you would infer. My wife simply discourages Christmas which is an entirely different matter.' So saying Shaun Baun feinted, snorted, shuffled and finally landed a nose-breaking blow which saw the drunkard fall to the ground with a cry of pain. At once Shaun Baun extended a helping hand and brought him to his feet where he assured him that full retribution had been extracted and that the matter was closed.

'However,' Shaun Baun drew himself up to his full height which was five feet one and a half inches, 'if you so much as look at my wife from this day forth I will break both your legs.'

The drunkard nodded his head eagerly, earnestly indicating that he had taken the warning to heart. He would, in the course of time, intimidate other women but he would never thereafter have anything to do with Polly Baun. For her part Polly would never know that an assault had taken place. Shaun would never tell her. She would only disapprove. She would continue to discourage Christmas as was her wont and, with this in mind, she decided to remove all the chairs from the kitchen and place them in the backyard until Christmas had run its course. If, she quite rightly deduced, there were no chairs for those who made Christmas visits they would not be able to sit down and, therefore, their visits would be of short duration.

On the day before Christmas Eve the hat shop was busy. Occasionally when a purchase was made the wearer would first defer to Polly's judgement. This, of course, necessitated a trip to the kitchen. The practice had been in existence for years. Countrymen in particular and confirmed bachelors would make the short trip to the kitchen to have their hats or caps inspected. On getting the nod from Polly Baun they would return to the shop and pay Shaun Baun for their purchases. Sometimes Polly would disapprove of the colour and other times she would disapprove of the shape. There were times when she would shake her head because of the hat's size or because of its rim or because of its crown. Shaun Baun's trade flourished because his customers were satisfied and the shy ones and the retiring ones and the irresolute ones left the premises safe in the knowledge that they would not be laughed at because of their choice of headgear.

As time passed and it became clear that the union would not be blessed with children Polly Baun became known as the woman who hated Christmas. Nobody would ever say it to her face and certainly nobody would say it to her husband's face. It must be said on behalf of the community that none took real exception to her stance. They were well used to Christmas attitudes. There was a tradesman who resided in the suburbs and every year about a week before Christmas he would disappear into the countryside where he rented a small cabin until Christmas was over. He had nothing personal against Christmas and had said so publicly on numerous occasions. It was just that he couldn't stand the build-up to Christmas what with the decorations and the lighting and the cards and the shopping and the gluttony to mention but a few of his grievances.

There was another gentleman who locked his door on Christmas Eve and did not open it for a month. Some say he simply hibernated and when he reappeared on the street after the prescribed period he looked as if he had. He was unshaven and his hair was tousled and his face was gaunt as a corpse's and there were black circles under his eyes.

Then there were those who would go off the drink for Christmas just because everybody else was going on. And there were those who would not countenance seasonal fare such as turkeys or geese or plum pudding or spiced beef. One man said he would rather an egg and another insisted that those who consumed fowl would have tainted innards for the rest of their days.

There were, therefore, abundant precedents for attitudes like Polly Baun's. There were those who would excuse her on the grounds that maybe she had a good and secret reason to hate Christmas but mostly they would accept what Shaun said, that she simply discouraged it.

There had been occasions when small children would come to the door of the kitchen while their parents searched for suitable hats. The knowing ones would point to where the silhouette of the woman who hated Christmas was visible through the stained glass of the doorway which led from the shop to the kitchen. One might whisper to the others as he pointed inwards 'that's the woman who hates Christmas!' If Polly Baun heard, she never reacted. Sometimes in the streets, during the days before Christmas, she would find herself the object of curious stares from shoppers who had just been informed of her pet aversion by friends or relations. If she noticed she gave no indication.

Shaun Baun also felt the seasonal undercurrents when he visited his neighbourhood tavern during the Christmas festivities. He drank but little, a few glasses of stout with a friend but never whiskey. He had once been a prodigious whiskey drinker and then all of a sudden he gave up whiskey altogether and never indulged again. No one knew why, not even his closest friends. There was no explanation. One night he went home full of whiskey and the next night he drank none. There was the inevitable speculation but the truth would never be known and his friends, all too well aware of his fiery temper, did not pursue the matter. Neither did they raise the question of his wife's Christmas disposition except when his back was turned but like most of the community they did not consider it to be of any great significance. There was, of course, a reason for it. There had to be if one accepted the premise that there was a reason for everything.

On Christmas Eve there was much merriment and good-will in the tavern. Another of Shaun Baun's cronies had given up whiskey on his doctor's instructions and presumed wrongly that this might well have been the reason why Shaun had forsaken the stuff. Courteously but firmly Shaun informed him that his giving up whiskey had nothing to do with doctors, that it was a purely personal decision. The night was spoiled for Shaun Baun. Rather than betray his true feelings on such an occasion he slipped away early and walked as far as the outermost suburbs of the town, then turned and made his way homewards at a brisk pace. Nobody could be blamed for thinking that here was a busy shopkeeper availing himself of the rarer airs of the night whereas the truth was that his mind was in turmoil, all brought on by the reference to whiskey in the public house. Nobody knew better than Shaun why he had given up whiskey unless it was his wife.

As he walked he clenched and unclenched his fists and cursed the day that he had ever tasted whiskey. He remembered striking her and he remembered why and as he did he stopped and threw his arms upwards into the night and sobbed as he always sobbed whenever he found himself unable to drive the dreadful memory away. He remembered how he had been drinking since the early afternoon on that fateful occasion. Every time he sold a hat he would dash across the roadway to the pub with the purchaser in tow. He reckoned afterwards that he had never consumed so much whiskey in so short a time. When he closed the shop he announced that he was going straight to the public house and this despite his wife's protestations. She begged him to eat something. She lovingly entreated him not to drink any more whiskey, to indulge in beer or stout and he agreed and kissed her and then hurried off to surfeit himself with more whiskey. He would later excuse himself on the grounds that he was young and impetuous but he would never be able to excuse the use of his fist in that awful moment which would haunt him for the rest of his life. An oncoming pedestrian moved swiftly on to the roadway at the sight of the gesticulating creature who seemed to rant and rave as he approached. Shaun Baun moved relentlessly onward, trying to dispel the memory of what had been the worst moment he had ever experienced but he still remembered as though it had happened only the day before.

He had left the pub with several companions and they had gone on to an after-hours establishment where they exceeded themselves. Shaun had come home at seven o'clock in the morning. He searched in vain for his key but it was nowhere to be found. He turned out his pockets but the exercise yielded nothing. Then he did what his likes had been doing since the first key had been mislaid. He knocked gently upon the front window with his knuckles and when this failed to elicit a response he located a coin and used it to beat a subdued tattoo on the fanlight and when this failed he pounded upon the door.

At length the door was opened to him and closed behind him by his dressing-gowned, bedroom-slippered wife. It took little by way of skill to evade his drunken embrace. She passed him easily in the shop and awaited him with folded arms in the kitchen.

A wiser woman would have ushered him upstairs, bedded him safely down and suspended any verbal onslaught until a more favourable time. She did not know so early in her married days that the most futile of all wifely exercises is arguing with a drunken husband.

She began by asking him if he saw the state of himself which was a pointless question to begin with. She asked him in short order if he knew the hour of the morning it was and was he aware of the fact that he was expected to accompany her to mass in a few short hours. He stood silently, hands and head hanging, unable to muster a reply. All he wished for was his bed; even the floor would have satisfied him but she had only begun. She outlined for him all the trouble he had caused her in their three years of marriage, his drinking habits, his bouts of sickness after the excesses of the pub, his intemperate language and, worst of all, the spectacle he made of himself in front of the neighbours. Nothing remarkable here, the gentle reader would be sure to say, familiar enough stuff and common to such occasions in the so-called civilised countries of the world but let me stress that it was not the quality of her broadsides but the quantity. She went on and on and on and it became clear that she should have vented her ire piecemeal over the three years rather than hoard it all for one sustained outburst.

Afterwards Shaun Baun would say that he did what he did to shut out the noise. If there had been lulls now and then he might have borne it all with more patience but she simply never let up. On the few occasions that he nodded off she shouted into the more convenient ear so that he would splutter into immediate if drunken wakefulness. Finally, the whole business became unbearable. Her voice had reached its highest pitch since the onslaught began and she even grew surprised at the frenzy of her own outpourings.

Could she but have taken a leaf out of the books of the countless wives in the neighbourhood who found themselves confronted with equally intemperate spouses she would have fared much better and there would be no need for recrimination on Christmas morning. Alas, this was not her way. She foolishly presumed that the swaying monstrosity before her was one of a kind and that a drastic dressing-down of truly lasting proportions was his only hope of salvation.

Whenever he tried to move out of earshot she seized him firmly by the shoulders and made him stand his ground. Drunk and incapable as he was he managed to place the table between them. For awhile they played a game of cat and mouse but eventually he tired and she began a final session of ranting which had the effect of clouding his judgment such was its intensity. He did not realise that he had delivered the blow until she had fallen to the ground.

Afterwards he would argue with himself that he only meant to remove her from his path so that he could escape upstairs and find succour in the spare bedroom. She fell heavily, the blood streaming from a laceration on her cheekbone. When he attempted to help her he fell awkwardly across her and stunned himself when his forehead struck the floor. When he woke he saw that the morning's light was streaming in the window. The clock on the kitchen mantelpiece confirmed his worst fears. For the first time in his life he had missed mass. Then slowly the events of the night before began to take shape.

He prayed in vain that he had experienced a nightmare, that his wife would appear any moment bouncing and cheerful from last mass. He struggled to his feet and entered his shop.

The last of the mass-goers had departed the street outside. Fearing the worst he climbed the stairs to the bedroom which they had so lovingly shared since they first married. She lay on the bed her head propped up by bloodstained pillows, a plaster covering the gash she had suffered, her face swollen beyond belief. Shaun Baun fell on his knees at the side of the bed and sobbed his very heart out but the figure on the bed lay motionless, her unforgiving eyes fixed on the ceiling. There would be no Christmas dinner on that occasion. Contritely, all day and all night, he made sobbing visitations to the bedroom with cups of coffee and tea and other beverages but there was to be no relenting.

Three months would pass before she acknowledged his existence and three more would expire before words were exchanged. Two years in all would go unfleetingly by before it could be said that they had the semblance of a relationship. That had all been twenty-five years before and now as he walked homewards avoiding the main streets he longed to kneel before her and beg her forgiveness once more. Every so often during the course of every year in between he would ask her to forgive the unforgivable as he called it. He had never touched her in anger since that night or raised his voice or allowed his face to exhibit the semblance of a frown in her presence.

When he returned she was sitting silently by the fire. The goose, plucked and stuffed, sat on a large dish. It would be duly roasted on the morrow. As soon as he entered the kitchen he sat by her side and took her hand in his. As always, he declared his love for her and she responded, as always, by squeezing the hand which held hers. They would sit thus as they had sat since that unforgettable night so many years before. There would be no change in the pattern. They would happily recall the events of the day and they would decide upon which mass they would attend on the great holy day. She would accept the glass of sherry which he always poured for her. He would pour himself a bottle of stout and they would sip happily. They would enjoy another drink and another and then they would sit quietly for awhile. Then as always the sobbing would begin. It would come from deep within him. He would kneel in front of her with his head buried in her lap and every so often, between great heaving sobs, he would tell her how sorry he was. She would nod and smile and place her hands around his head and then he would raise the head and look into her eyes and ask her forgiveness as he had been doing for so many years.

'I forgive you dear,' she would reassure him and he would sob all the more. She would never hurt him. She could not find it in her heart to do that. He was a good man if a hotheaded one and he had made up for that moment of madness many times over. All through the night she would dutifully comfort him by accepting his every expression of atonement. She always thought of her father on such occasions. He had never raised his voice to her or to her mother. He had been drunk on many an occasion, notably weddings and christenings but all he ever did was to lift her mother or herself in his arms. She was glad that she was able to forgive her husband but there was forgiveness and forgiveness and hers was the kind that would never let her forget. Her husband would never know the difference. She would always be there when he needed her, especially at Christmas.

PAIL BUT NOT WAN

ONE OF MY FONDEST MEMORIES OF CHRISTMAS is a whistling milkman now passed on to that sweet clime where whistle the gentle winds of heaven. He would whistle louder, longer and sweeter at Christmas than at any other time of the year.

He must have been sixty when I first heard him of a Christmas morning many years ago. He was a curly-haired, chubby-faced fellow who looked only thirty years of age, although in reality he was double that age. He was that kind of person. Age, it would seem, made no impression on him.

Without doubt his fountain of youth was his whistling. First thing in the morning after the cocks had crowed and the last of the crows flown countrywards his exhilarating serenading could be heard clearly for long distances as he cycled upon his rounds.

What a happy man he must have been! He never whistled a drab melody. He excelled most of all at the stirring march and he would generously empty his heart to all and sundry at no charge whatsoever. Romantic airs were meat and drink to him and he would give his all in an effort to strum the sweet chords of love which lie dormant in so many people.

Dour veterans of the marital confrontation would relent

and turn in their beds to celebrate sweet sessions of amorous rapture and all because of his incidental input. No nightingale ever sang so sweetly as he. No skylark ever plumbed the soulful depths for sensitive melody. The early morning, ushered in by the waning stars, was merely the backdrop for his princely renditions.

He contributed more to the rescue of foundering marriages than any human intermediary could ever hope to. It often seemed that he was especially transported from some heavenly sphere for no other purpose than the upraising of downcast hearts. Even his lightweight warblings would fritter away depressions and lift up the human spirit to its loftiest pinnacles.

Surely the pipings of that yesterday milkman had their origins in heaven although it was the orifice of his contracting lips that modulated and measured the bewitching torrent of empyrean sonority which charmed and delighted all those who happened to be within earshot. There wasn't a child in the street who did not try to emulate that dear, departed milkman.

I remember once of an icy morning before Christmas he fell from his rickety bicycle, spilling the contents of both his pails and breaking two front teeth into the bargain. His lips, poor fellow, were brutally lacerated. The tears formed in his eyes as he witnessed the streams of freshly-drawn milk coursing irredeemably to the nearest channel but how quickly did he transform misfortune into triumph.

Supporting himself on his right knee and placing his left hand over his breast he pursed his shattered lips, oblivious to the agonising pain. Then extending his right hand to his unseen public he gave the performance of his life. Long before he finished, the under-employed lips of couples in that once dreary street were never so utilised in the pursuit of loving fulfilment. For the listening lovers in the silent houses it was a never-to-be-forgotten experience. Some had never even dreamed of aspiring to such unprecedented ecstasies. Many had waited a score of Christmases for such a development.

If only the world and its people could wait long enough everybody would eventually be kissed by someone, be loved by someone.

This piece is just an informal salute to Christmas and to the memory of a forgotten milkman who made life more harmonious on a far-off Christmas morning for those within his round.

THE GOOD
CORNER BOY

THIS IS THE STORY OF THE GOOD corner boy. As stories go it is as
true as any. To some it may seem improbable but I can counter
this by stating that most true stories seem that way anyway.
Enough, however, of the preamble. Let us proceed without
further ado.

On 20 December 1971, Madgie Crane withdrew some of
her savings from the bank. A tidy sum was involved; two hundred pounds no less but then as she might say herself she had
many calls. There were sons and daughters and grandchildren. There were neighbours and there were friends and relations. Of husbands she had none. There had been one but he
had passed on some years before and she had come to terms
with her grief in the course of time.

As she turned the corner which would take her to the post
office she bumped accidentally into another woman who
chanced to be returning from the same venue. As a result Madgie Crane's purse jumped from the grocery bag where it had
been securely wedged between a cabbage and a half-pound of
rashers. It landed at the feet of the corner boy in residence and
that worthy immediately fenced it between his waiting boots
where no trace of it remained visible to the searching eye.

The minutes passed but no move did our corner boy make. He looked hither and thither from time to time but if there had never been a purse between his feet he would have looked hither and thither anyway and he would have looked up and down anyway but he would never have bent to tie his shoes for in all the years that I have spent studying corner boys I never saw one bend to tie his shoes.

As he pretended to look after his laces his delicate fingers quickly opened the purse and his drowsy eyes looked inside. Two hundred pounds if there was a penny! Deftly he flicked the purse up the loose sleeve of his faded raincoat and rose to his feet. Even if somebody had been watching, and he was sure that nobody had, his actions could not possibly convey anything of a disingenuous nature.

It was no more than a formality to insert his hands into his trousers pockets with the purse still up his sleeve. A gentle shake of the sleeve in question and the purse fell downwards into the waiting pocket. It was precisely at that moment that he was addressed by Madgie Crane. There was a tear in her eye and a quiver in her voice.

'I suppose,' she opened tremulously, 'you saw no sign of a purse.'

No answer came from the seemingly mystified corner boy. It was as though she had spoken in a strange tongue.

'Every penny I had was inside in it,' she continued.

Still no response from the resident corner boy. He blew his nose and he looked hither and thither. He shifted his weight from one foot to the other and he looked secondly at Madgie Crane. He noted the weariness and the confusion and he watched without change of expression as the tears became more copious. Her brimming eyes discharged them aplenty down the sides of her withered face. His hand tightened on the swollen purse and he inclined his head towards the channel which ran parallel to the pavement.

Hard as he would try afterwards he would never be able to explain why he did what he did because he needed money at that point in his life as he had never needed money before. He needed it for his widowed sister with whom he lodged and he needed it for her children who he loved and he needed it to pay his bills. He needed it so that he might embark on a comprehensive drunk for a day or two for he believed that this was his entitlement because of the season that was in it.

Having inclined his head towards a particular spot in the channel he moved swiftly in that direction and pretended to retrieve the purse. Lifting it aloft he enquired of Madgie Crane if this indeed was the missing article. Madgie chortled with delight and clapped her dumpling hands together soundlessly. She stood on her toes for the first time in twenty years and graciously accepted her property from the hands of her benefactor.

She opened the purse and she proceeded to count her money. Never was there such an assiduous reckoning and never did anyone count so little for so long. Assuring herself that every note was present and correct she instituted a second count and finally, when that was satisfactorily concluded, she started a third count. It was during the middle of this count that she moved off in the direction of the post office where she had deposited her grocery bag with an obliging clerk.

The corner boy stood amazed. He had been stunned and shocked many times in his life but he had never been amazed.

It was a strange and unnerving experience for a man of his years. A giddiness assailed him and he collapsed in an ungainly heap at the corner where he had stood rocklike for so long.

A half hour later he woke up in a nearby public house just as an ambulance arrived on the scene. He refused all forms of aid and was told that a doctor was on the way. He declined the publican's offer to wait in the snug but he did not decline the medicinal brandy tendered to him by the publican's wife. Exactly forty-five minutes after his collapse he returned to his corner and took up his usual position.

Word of his good deed spread and the community was shocked to learn that he had received nothing by way of reward from Madgie Crane. No wonder he fainted, some said and he was right to faint, more said. An ad hoc committee was formed and a collection made. It amounted to eleven pounds two shillings and seven pence half-penny. He wrapped it in his handkerchief and instructed a neighbour who chanced to be passing to deliver it to his sister. For the rest of the day, because it was Christmas time, he answered all queries from passers by, directing strangers to the post office, the banks and the churches, often accompanying them to the extremes of his bailiwick and imparting his blessing on all. Also because it was Christmas he led the old and the feeble across the busy roadway, cautioning them to alert him whenever they wished to cross back again. Only at Christmas do corner boys involve themselves in the activities around them.

Then a second giddiness assailed him but this time it was accompanied by a sharp pain in the chest. He fell to the pavement where he immediately expired. When word of his passing spread, all who knew him agreed that he had been a good

corner boy. He never scolded children and he was the last refuge of wandering tomcats who took shelter behind him at
night when cross canines might tear them asunder. He was devoted to his corner. Those who knew him would testify that he
lived for nothing else and that it was because of his corner he
never married.

When drunkards fought or scuffled on their way homewards he never interfered, thereby assuring the impoverished
and the curious of free entertainment unlike others who spoiled the fun by coming between the contestants. His corner
would never be the same again nor would we look upon his
likes again. Truly it could be said that he died at his post and
surely it would be right and fitting to call him the good corner
boy.

SOMETHING DRASTIC

CANON CORNELIUS COODLE STOOD WITH HIS PALMS on the parapet of Ballybradawn bridge and surveyed the swirling, foaming flood waters below. The Canon could never cross any bridge at home or abroad without pausing to inspect the waters that passed beneath. He had once been a salmon angler and was locally regarded as something of an authority on lures, particularly artificial flies and minnows which he frequently made himself. He was of the belief that every major river needed its own particular bait.

Generally speaking suitable baits were to be found in shops which catered for the needs of anglers but because of the contours of local river beds and because of the related agitation of the changing waters the Canon believed that one had to be specific. There were other factors too such as the light and shade peculiar to certain stretches of water influenced by the arboreal canopies at particular times of year. All of these and many other features, too numerous to mention, had to be taken into account when a man sat down to prepare his angling gear for the beginning of the angling season which was no more than ten days away.

Canon Coodle had not fished for several years. Now in his

early eighties he lacked the sprightliness which once saw him vault the most formidable of stiles in his stride and leap unerringly from rock to crag to grassy inch where a false step might easily mean permanent immersion or at the very least a broken limb.

As he looked down the river's course he recalled doughty salmon which he had landed in his heyday. A happy smile crossed his face but was at once replaced by a frown for which he could find no apparent justification. This was the worrying part. His memory had started to fail him as well as his physical agility and he wondered what it might be that had occasioned the frown. In vain he tried to bring it to mind. He knew for certain that there was a problem and undoubtedly it was an unpleasant task and it would hang over him until it presented itself at the most unlikely and unfavourable time such as when he might be sitting in his study after dinner smoking his pipe or savouring a sip from the glass of port in which he sometimes indulged after a satisfactory meal. Then the forgotten obligation or predicament would intrude not because he would remember it of his own accord but because it would be thrust upon him by a reminder from his housekeeper or curates or by a visit from the person or persons involved.

Always when making a promise that he would perform a particular function he would start right away in the direction of his study to make a note of the business but by the time he reached pencil and paper he would have forgotten. He was a prudent enough man about the maintenance of his health so that when he found the chill of the river winds penetrating his overcoat he began his return journey to the presbytery.

Every evening before dinner he would walk briskly as far

as the bridge and back again. He never dawdled on such excursions. The pangs of hunger and the prospect of an excellent dinner saw to that. It was the only business, apart from celebration of his masses, of which his housekeeper did not need to remind him. It was said of him that he had a good stroke which simply meant in the everyday idiom of the place that he was possessed of a healthy appetite.

Upon his return he knelt for awhile in prayer. Then came the persistent tinkling of the housekeeper's bell. After a decent interval he joined his curates in the dining-room. Throughout the excellent meal the talk centred on Christmas duties. It was during dessert that the younger of the curates reminded the Canon that he was expected at the local convent at two o'clock on Christmas Day where, as had been the custom for the eighteen years of his canonship, he would be expected to join the sisters for the Christmas dinner.

The curate had been waylaid by Mother Francesca, a towering figure of commensurate girth for whom both curates and their beloved pastor had a healthy respect if not regard.

'Was she born a reverend mother,' a wisecracking bishop had once asked, 'because,' he continued, 'I just cannot imagine her as a novice.'

It would be true to say, however, that Francesca was not as bad as she was painted. All she ever wanted was her own way and as long as that was forthcoming life could be tolerable enough for those who came into contact with her on a regular basis. So that was it then, the Canon relieved after a fashion, pushed away his half-finished dessert and declined the offer of coffee from the senior curate. At the mention of Francesca's name and the awful prospect of the Christmas dinner which he could not avoid he had instantly decided that instead of the glass of port to which he would normally address himself he would finish off the bottle which contained, in his humble estimation, at least three glasses. He felt it was his inalienable right in view of what he would have to suffer shortly as a consequence of parochial custom.

After the port he would go straight to bed for, as he well knew, he would be in no condition to go anywhere else. His curates no longer allowed him to go on sick calls after dark unless it was a special occasion and then only if one of the curates was available to transport him.

The younger men had noted his reaction when reminded of his unwelcome seasonal responsibility. They had both dined with Mother Francesca and they had both been obliged to resort to Vesuvian belches in order to get rid of the trapped winds and obnoxious gases which had built up to dangerous levels after the meals which Francesca insisted on preparing herself, especially if those invited to dine were members of the clergy. She had been brought up to believe that the clergy needed and were entitled to richer, meatier and generally more substantial meals than lay people no matter how pious. The official convent cook, Sister Carmelita, never interfered when her superior became involved. She had been tempted often enough especially during the preparation for the Christmas dinner but like all the other inmates she opted for the peaceful way out and kept her mind to herself.

Christmas, which was not the norm for Christmas days in that part of the world, broke mild and balmy and belied the time of year that was in it. The presbytery housekeeper had taken off at first light on her bicycle for her sister's home in the nearby hills and, after the masses, the curates would head for the homes of their families in the north and south of the diocese.

The Canon would look after the sick calls, if any, and one of the curates would return before darkness to relieve the Canon who would be in no fit mental condition to go anywhere, anyway, after his ordeal at the convent and it was to this venerable institution that he wended his way shortly before two o'clock on the appointed day to partake of the Christmas fare so lovingly prepared by Mother Francesca.

During Francesca's brief absences from the kitchen Sister Carmelita would furtively and speedily modify the more distasteful aspects of the reverend mother's preparations. 'Otherwise she might poison us all!' she told herself not without justification.

As Canon Coodle drew near the tree-lined entrance his steps faltered and he cast about him that sort of despairing look which was to be seen on the faces of condemned souls as they ascend the steps to the gallows. Although he tried to banish them, visions of the previous years' dinners began to take shape before his mind's eye. How could he ever forget the monumental heap which covered the huge dish so that not a solitary speck of the esteemed willow pattern was to be seen anywhere beneath. There was, to begin with, a mound of mashed turnips which would comfortably cope with the needs of a small hotel for the round of a day and there was a mighty heap of potato stuffing which would go a long way towards assuaging the hunger pangs of the average family with a grandparent or two thrown in for good measure.

There had been peas and beans, white meat and dark as

well as the outsized thigh of the largest cock turkey that could be found in the countryside for miles around and all of this on the same plate, covered with fat-infused gravy. Worst of all, the victims were expected to consume every trace of food on their plates. The Canon shuddered at the memory. Mother Francesca always took it as a personal affront if anybody failed to clear the plate. She eschewed containers for the different vegetables stoutly maintaining that there was too much trouble involved and that, anyway, it was nothing more than grandiose nonsense.

All her charges from young postulants to elderly sisters who had all but forgotten where they originally came from had the foresight to cut down on food intake for days before and especially on Christmas morning with such a challenge looming in front of them. The Canon had expressly foregone breakfast so that he would be capable of making inroads into Francesca's plate not to mention her specially enriched plum pudding which followed hot on the heels of the monstrous main course. The plum pudding in turn was followed by Christmas cake and several freshly opened tins of assorted biscuits which had to be liberally sampled and seen to be liberally sampled.

The saddest aspect of the entire orgy as far as Canon Cornelius Coodle was concerned was that not a single drop of intoxicating drink was on display although it would have to be said that this was not entirely the fault of the reverend mother. Rather was it the fault of the Canon's predecessor Canon Montague and the reverend mother's predecessor Mother Amabilis.

The late Canon Montague, poor fellow, had the reputation

of being the heaviest drinker in the diocese and would drink any other two clerics under the table, at any given sitting, without exerting himself. His friend Mother Amabilis was what locals would call an innocent sort, that is to say she was a trifle naive as far as the ways of the world were concerned. She would ply the late Canon with his favourite poison, Hooter's Heart-throb whiskey until, I turn to the locals again, it came out through his eyes.

Always, by the time the dinner ended he was incapable of negotiating the journey from convent to presbytery of his own accord. Before he expired at the astonishing age of eighty-nine from sheer senility and a perfectly functioning liver, he had consumed a veritable reservoir of Hooter's Heart-throb. On the Christmas of his eighty-sixth year he was so plied with his favourite tincture by Mother Amabilis that he was unable to perform his priestly duties for three whole days. Word inevitably reached the bishop of the diocese and, as a consequence, the mother-general paid a surprise visit to Mother Amabilis shortly after Christmas or to be exact on the afternoon of the feast of the Epiphany. She called her aside, as it were, and from that moment forth an embargo was placed on intoxicating drink within the confines of the convent. All existing stocks were transferred to the local hospital where they might be used in moderation for purely medicinal purposes.

Oddly enough Canon Coodle placed not a particle of blame on his otherwise illustrious predecessor or on the open-handed Mother Amabilis. There is none of us who does not suffer in some small way from the sins of our ancestors but the balance is nearly always redressed by the goodness they leave behind.

Canon Coodle, with apologies to none, fortified himself, to a limited degree, by imbibing two glasses of twelve year old whiskey prior to his departure for the convent and he now found himself flushed of face but sound in mind and limb, with no prospect of further drink, at the hall door of the convent. He was warmly received and it must be said that there wasn't a nun there, Mother Francesca apart, who would not have gladly lifted the cruel restriction given the authority to do so. There was no doubt but that Mother Francesca had the power to do so because the present incumbent of the bishopric would have yielded to any demand she might make rather than incur her ire.

Francesca, alas, had been born of drunken parents and since there are some who believe that it is better to be born in hell there was no way she would countenance the lifting of the ban on alcohol. Rather than possessing a genuine vocation for her calling the reverend mother was a refugee from the real world and like all refugees she was so thankful to be in a safe haven that she would rather die than invalidate an established procedure.

As the nuns tripped merrily into the spacious dining-room the Canon trudged behind escorted by Mother Francesca. They sat according to rank and age along both sides of the table with the Canon at the head and the reverend mother at the bottom.

All present then reverentially entwined their fingers and sat rigidly as they waited for the Canon to start the proceedings with the Grace Before Meals. He had but barely concluded when the phone rang. All sat silently in the hope that it would go away but go it did not. Mother Francesca lifted her mighty frame slowly from her seat. What a rugby forward she would have made, the Canon almost laughed aloud, if she had been born of the opposite sex although as she bore down upon the offending phone she looked more like a battleship. A heated argument ensued. It was obvious that the person at the other end of the line was determined to have her way.

'Can't it wait a half hour?' the Reverend Mother shouted. Her frown suggested that the answer was in the negative.

'But he's just about to begin his Christmas dinner, poor man,' the Reverend Mother persisted vehemently. The anger on her face as she listened intimated that the caller did not really care what the Canon was sitting down to.

'All right, all right!' the Reverend Mother called at the top of her voice, 'we'll let him decide for himself.'

Meanwhile Canon Cornelius Coodle, vicar general of the diocese and the eldest of its priests, had been an eager listener. Was the possibility of a reprieve on the cards?

'You are required for a sick call,' Mother Francesca spoke as if the Canon was to blame, 'but I have suggested to this person,' she distastefully indicated the mouthpiece in her hand, 'that you be allowed finish your dinner first.'

The Canon rose to his feet, touching the sides of his mouth with the large white napkin provided by his hosts in an effort to conceal his absolute delight.

'Find out where it is,' he asked gently, 'we must never keep a poor soul waiting.' He laid the napkin on the table and blessed himself although he had neither sipped nor eaten.

'You won't believe this,' the Reverend Mother turned her attention to the nuns who had been highly entertained by the exchanges, 'but they want him to go to the very top of Ballybuggawn at his age without a bite inside in him.' All the nuns tut-tutted obediently and reproachfully.

'I'll have to fetch my car,' the Canon was already moving towards the door of the dining-room, his face alight with joy, a surging youthfulness in his step.

'Wait, wait!' Mother Francesca called after him. 'The sisters will drive you as far as your car and you can take your dinner with you.' Here she summoned the younger members of her community and in no time at all a pair of eager sisters appeared from the kitchen with a large wickerwork basket containing the delights already mentioned.

'No need, no need,' the Canon raised his hands aloft. It required his best efforts to control his happiness. He wanted to leap, to shout, to dance while Mother Francesca lifted the white cloth which covered the massive array of goodies which they had prepared for him. He feigned inexpressible gratitude and announced that he would do justice to the fare before the night was out. Then he was gone followed by the two nuns who bore the basket between them. They would deposit it in the boot of his car on his instructions and he would proceed airily to Flanagan's of Ballybuggawn and, if it was on top of the highest hill in the parish itself, he wouldn't have minded were it twice as high or the road twice as dangerous. He was a free man and, more importantly, a clergyman on his way to succour some unfortunate soul who desperately needed forgiveness. Otherwise why would he or she seek the services of a priest on Christmas Day?

Canon Coodle regretted that he would not be able to keep his promise about doing justice to the contents of the basket but he promised himself that it would not be thrown away untouched. With this in mind he drew to a halt near an iron gate which led to a green field half-way up the hill of Ballybuggawn. A large flock of crows had just alighted thereon and who better to consume and relish an unwanted meal than the birds of the air. Entering the field, basket in hand, he looked all around to see if anybody was watching. He need not have worried. Man, woman and child in the area were sitting down to dinner or had finished dinner and were resting.

Then, hastily, he unceremoniously dumped the entire convent dinner and returned each plate to the basket before returning to his car. Nobody would ever know and when Mother Francesca would ask if he had enjoyed his Christmas dinner he could truthfully reply that it had gone down well and there wasn't a single one of the crows, already gorging themselves with delighted squawks, who would contradict him. He stood contentedly, hands clasped behind back, surveying the snow-covered summit of Ballybuggawn. He brought his hands to his midriff and entwined them prayerfully as he expressed his gratitude to the Lord of creation for his happy lot. If, at the end of his days, he should be asked to nominate the happiest day of his life he would have no hesitation in selecting the day that was in it.

At Flanagan's of Ballybuggawn he was well received. Here in this humble cot he was respected above all other men in the parish for his humility and saintliness. Joe and Sarah Flanagan, a childless couple in their late seventies were mystified when the Canon asked to be shown into the presence of the sick party. As the elderly pair continued to exchange baffled looks the Canon announced that he would administer the sacrament of Extreme Unction without further delay.

'I'm afraid there's been a mistake Canon,' Joe Flanagan forestalled him, 'there's nobody sick here.'

Joe's wife Sarah curtsied and spoke next. 'We haven't been sick a day thank God these fifty years Canon,' she said proudly.

'And is there another Flanagan in the neighbourhood?' the Canon asked politely.

He was informed with equal politeness that he was looking at the only two Flanagans on Ballybuggawn Hill from top to bottom.

'And is there anybody in need of a priest hereabouts?' the Canon ventured. No. There was nobody sick in the vicinity thank God but might it not be some other Flanagan in some other part of the parish?

'Oh dear, oh dear!' Canon Coodle looked out through the small window of the kitchen and saw that the first stars were beginning to appear prematurely as dusk embraced the snow-crested hill.

'It's a long journey back to town Canon,' Joe Flanagan reminded his parish priest.

'And a cold one Canon,' Sarah Flanagan was curtsying again.

'Would you take a drop of something Canon,' Joe Flanagan asked in a most respectful tone, 'a tint of the hot stuff now for the journey?'

'Or there's port,' Sarah put in, 'Sandeman's Five Star or there's brandy if you'd care for it?'

'Port,' the Canon divested himself of his overcoat and took the chair which Joe had moved closer to the fire, 'a port would be much appreciated.'

An hour later after the Canon had swallowed a large glass of port and eaten two boiled eggs with several slices of home-made brown bread the trio knelt and recited the Rosary after which the Canon thanked his hosts from the bottom of his heart and assured them that he had never eaten such flavoursome eggs or such nourishing bread in his entire life.

The trio had concluded earlier that the Canon had been the victim of a mischievous joke and privately the Canon could not find it in his heart to condemn the mischief-maker if such indeed it was. Reluctantly he took his leave and promised faithfully that he would visit for his supper again when the snow had departed from the hilltop and the slopes brightened by the lengthening days.

That night in the presbytery sitting-room the Canon sat with his two curates and housekeeper. Between sips of port he recounted the events of the day but made no reference to the convent basket or the delighted crows. He waxed eloquently about the simple but incomparable fare given with such a heart and a will by the Flanagans.

'There is nothing on the face of creation,' the housekeeper said solemnly, 'as good as a free-range egg, freshly laid.' Her listeners lifted their glasses in agreement while she rearranged the knitting which lay upon her lap. 'What crowns it all, of course, is fresh-brown bread made with expert hands and Sarah Flanagan has years of bread-making behind her.'

Again the listeners lifted their glasses, this time without drinking from them.

'But,' the housekeeper was continuing as she resumed her knitting, 'if there was home-made butter going with the brown bread you would have a feast fit for a parish priest.'

Here they all laughed, none more so than the Canon. The housekeeper smiled to herself when the laughter had abated. She had made the call from her sister's phone and she had adopted a sharp Ulster accent in an effort to conceal her identity. There was no doubt in her mind that she had escaped detection. She had no qualms of conscience about the call. Her primary role in life was to protect her Canon against all-comers whether bishops, mutinous curates, rampaging reverend mothers or whosoever threatened the Canon's well-being. Other executives in the lay world had wives and secretaries to look out for them whereas Canon Coodle, on the threshold of infirmity, was easy prey for assorted parochial predators. She had watched him suffer over the years at the indelicate hands of Mother Francesca, a pampered virago, who couldn't fry a sausage properly and who had burned more rashers in her time than any ten women in the parish put together. Of late the housekeeper had noticed a slight decline in the Canon's health, especially during the days leading up to Christmas when she knew that the awful prospect of Francesca's cooking was about as much as he could bear. She had made up her mind irreversibly before she left for her sister's on Christmas Day. Nobody else seemed to notice the extreme distress of Canon Coodle. She resolved that something drastic should be done and that she was the one to do it. She knew Joe and Sarah Flanagan as well as she could know anybody. She knew of their genuine regard for Canon Coodle and she knew that the Flanagans would see to his welfare foodwise. She was proud of what she had done. She had won a reprieve for her lord and master and now that the precedent had been established she would ensure that he would never again have to endure the murderous concoctions of Francesca and thus guarantee a longer and less stressful life for her ageing parish priest.

THE WOMAN
WHO PASSED
HERSELF OUT

JENNY COLLINS HAD A PHILOSOPHY ABOUT CHRISTMAS. She shared
it with her friends and neighbours as she did with everything
else she had.

'Christmas,' said Jenny, 'is like an egg. If you don't take it
before its date of expiry it will turn rotten.' The trouble with
Jenny was that she took her own words too much to heart. For
instance she would send out greeting cards from the middle of
October onwards. This would be acceptable if the cards were
destined for such far-off places as Tristan da Cunha or Faiza-
bad but the opposite was nearly always the case. Mostly the
cards were for neighbours or for friends who lived nearby. Occasionally there would be one addressed to Dublin or Cork,
places to where delivery was assured after a day or two.

'Jenny,' her father had said to her once after she served
him his Christmas dinner at eleven in the morning, 'you are in
mortal danger of passing yourself out.'

It was widely believed in that part of the world at that
time that those who passed themselves out rarely caught up
with themselves again. Jenny's father, who was in his eighties,
would explain to his friends that she brought the trait from her

101

grandmother who set out all her life for twelve o'clock mass at ten minutes past eleven and this despite the fact that the church was less than a hundred yards from her home. When the old lady eventually expired after a visit from the family doctor the latter was seen to shake his head in amazement when he was asked to pronounce her dead within the hour. He had predicted that she would hold out for at least a fortnight but true to form she had quit the land of the living fourteen days before her time. Her granddaughter Jenny had never been late for school and neither had any one of Jenny's three children, two girls and a boy who won every school attendance prize that was going and who were to be seen on all mass days with their parents in the front pew of the parish church at least a half hour before the priest and his retinue appeared at the altar. Others who were never in time for anything would shake their heads in disbelief at the folly of it all but Canon Coodle, the parish priest, was heard to say to his housekeeper that Jenny and her brood were to be commended.

'It is a holy and wholesome thought to pray for the dead,' the Canon said solemnly, 'so that they may be loosed from their sins.'

Jenny's husband Tom was of the strong silent variety. As far as he was concerned his wife's injunctions were law and, anyway, he was a most devout person. As well as that he seldom spoke and rarely contradicted. Jenny, therefore, was free to do as she pleased without previous consultations, not that she was ever likely to do anything untoward in the first place.

Older, wiser matrons along the street felt that Tom Collins should exercise a little more control over his wife's comings and goings on the grounds that it was not altogether correct to give a woman all the rein, especially a young woman. Be that as it may, as the man said, Jenny and Tom Collins were never at loggerheads and the children were healthy and happy.

Jenny's father who resided with them since his wife's death was well looked after although from time to time he would issue cautions to his daughter about the dangers of presumption and presupposition not to mention the awful consequences of passing herself out. He would issue these dire warnings on a daily basis as Christmas approached but he was too old and too infirm to realise that Jenny would have long beforehand anticipated Christmas. She would have scoured the shops near and far during the post Christmas and New Year's sales seasons in the hope of finding inexpensive but suitable presents for not-so-near relations and not-so-close friends. Then when the sales fever had worn off she would relax for a brief period but once Saint Patrick's Day had slipped by she would begin to feel the pressures of Christmas once more.

A suitable Sunday would be set aside so that she might engage two turkeys, one for Christmas and one for the feast of the Epiphany or the Women's Christmas as it was called thereabouts.

Sometime between the last week of March and the first week of April the entire family would fare forth on foot into the countryside as soon as the midday meal was consumed and the ware washed and dried. This particular excursion would always fall on a Sunday and so it happened that on the fifth Sunday of the Lenten period the family set out to the same farmhouse with the same Christmas order for turkeys, all five firmly wrapped against the wind and the rain. Jenny had seen to her father's wants before her departure and when she informed him of her plans he protested insisting that there was plenty of time with Christmas more than eight months away.

'And how do I know,' his daughter informed him, 'whether turkeys will be scarce or plentiful this coming Christmas and how do I know,' she went on, warming to her task, 'whether or not some disease might strike the turkey population between now and then and who's to say but a plague of foxes will not descend on the countryside and devour half the birds or who is to say what may or may not happen so isn't it better be sure than sorry?'

'Away with you,' he laughed extending his face for a kiss, 'you're every bit as bad as your grandmother.'

Secure in the knowledge that there would be turkeys for the distant festivities, Jenny Collins placed an order with her local butcher for spiced beef, standing close by to ensure that the order was properly entered in the appropriate ledger and that her name was spelled correctly.

Some would remark that it was just as well that she was not nearly so fastidious about other festivals. She would surely pass herself out altogether, they maintained, if she was. For instance she would not bother with shamrock for her husband's lapel or badges for her daughters coats until the very morning before Saint Patrick's Day nor would she bother with sprigs of palm for Palm Sunday until that very morning whereas others would have it ready, cut and blessed for days before. The simple truth was that Jenny Collins looked upon all other festivals as mere diversions on the road to Christmas.

Her father would agree.

'Jenny,' said he, 'sees the ending of one Christmas as the beginning of another. Personally speaking I do not wish to hear of Christmas until a week or so beforehand. It becomes diluted if it drags out too long. What's going to happen eventually is that they'll drag out Christmas so much that it will snap.'

Nobody took any notice of the old man and who could blame them! Had he not prophesied the end of the world three times and had not nothing happened! He was, it must be said, genuinely worried about his daughter.

'A lot of people do what I do,' she explained. 'It saves money and it saves time.'

He had shaken his head ominously at the time and would not be reassured. When Christmas finally came around Jenny Collins became nervous and fidgety and began to natter to herself when she thought nobody was listening.

Most of the time when we talk to ourselves we merely indulge in harmless quotes or we hum and we haw and vice versa. We do not, as Jenny Collins did, remind ourselves about the future. Quite unexpectedly she began to purchase odds and ends for the next Christmas despite the fact that the Christmas being celebrated was not yet over. Her father became greatly alarmed and went so far as to suggest that what Jenny was doing was sacrilegious. Her children, for the very first time, became worried and her husband decided it was time to speak. Is anything more eagerly awaited than the utterance of a man who has steadfastly kept his mouth shut over the years whilst others all around are pontificating! Consequently, when Tom Collins cleared his throat with a view towards expressing what could well be described as his maiden speech there was widespread alarm in the house. Jenny, anticipating a statement of unprecedented importance, called for order by rapping noisily on the milk jug with a dessert spoon. All the members of the family were seated at the table quite accidentally on the occasion. Jenny's father sat at the head completing his favourite crossword while his son-in-law Tom sat at the bottom with a face like a slipper trying to contain two blood-thirsty greyhounds who have just sighted a hare. He was waiting for precisely the right moment to unleash his two words. At one side sat Jenny and her son while at the other sat the two girls. The old man placed his crossword underneath the milk jug. The two girls put aside the text books with which they were involved. Son and mother jointly closed the history book which lay before them and Tom Collins cleared his throat for the second time.

'Bad business,' he said solemnly and although he was given all the time in the world he would not add further to the little he had already said. A silence ensued. It was a long silence during which everybody exchanged looks except the man whose statement had occasioned them.

Everybody present knew what Tom Collins meant. He was saying that while it was all right to plan one Christmas in advance it was not all right to plan two. The silence was allowed its allotted span before books were re-addressed and the crossword resumed. They were a wise family in that they knew there would be no point in saying any more.

Time passed and Jenny Collins wisely decided to celebrate one Christmas without reference to the second but only for awhile. The snows had but barely departed from the surrounding hills when a restlessness took hold of her. She was able to resist it for awhile but when the daffodils put in their appearance she began to have brief glimpses of future Christmases. She turned to prayer but her powers of concentration were no match for the urgings which seemed to redouble their efforts and as April bestrewed the shady places with delicate blooms she found it impossible to subdue the Christmas feelings to which she always had yielded in previous years and yet she did. She was to discover, however, that it is wrong to over-subdue for when the urge can no longer be held at bay it re-emerges with twice the power.

Jenny Collins went on a Christmas buying binge all through the last week of April. It appeared that she was making up for the time she had lost for instead of buying for just the Christmas ahead she bought for following Christmases as well. Surprised but considerate shop assistants would remind her that she had already bought certain items but she would explain that she was buying for an invalid friend. Normally she was not be given to untruths but she would excuse herself on the grounds that it was inventiveness rather than strict lying. Her husband was aware of what was going on and when she became aware that he was she was quick to point out that she wasn't squandering his money, that she would be spending it anyway sooner or later. He would say nothing. There would be no more pronouncements. The children took no notice. Adults could do what they liked and generally did.

As the summer sped by Jenny Collins bought more and more, inexpensive items mostly which she stored in the attic in an old chest.

'Not for the coming Christmas,' she explained to her

father, 'nor for the Christmas after but for future Christmases.'

'But where's the point?' her father had asked.

'Better be sure than sorry,' she had answered and when he expressed dissatisfaction with such a reply she had merely shrugged her shoulders and asked what harm if any she was doing.

'Things have come to a pretty pass,' her father scolded.

Later that night he invited his son-in-law to join him in a drink. They chose a quiet pub at the farthest end of the street. Half-way through the first drink the old man rounded on his son-in-law and asked somewhat petulantly: 'Why do you condone it?'

'I don't condone it,' came the considered response. 'I put up with it because she has no other fault and I figure that a woman needs one fault at least if she is to remain normal.'

'That's all very fine,' the old man said, 'but where will it all end! If she's not stopped soon she'll be buying ten or even twenty years ahead of normal.'

There was no immediate answer from Tom Collins. It was obvious that he had not contemplated this new aspect of the problem. He had no fault to find with Jenny but if what the old man had prophesied came to pass Jenny would have to be taken aside.

'I'll take her aside,' he promised.

'When?' the old man asked.

'One of these days now I'll get down to it.'

'Too late,' the old man shook his head ruefully and finished his drink. 'It is my considered opinion,' he looked his son-in-law in the eye, 'that she is in the process of passing herself out and, once they start, the trend becomes irreversible. I am not laying all the blame on you. I am also partly responsible.'

'What do we do?' Tom Collins asked anxiously.

'We will have to take drastic steps, that's what we'll have to do,' the old man answered.

'What do you mean!' Tom asked anxiously.

'I mean,' the old man became deadly serious, 'we shall have to enlist outside help.'

'But who?' his son-in-law asked.

'The parish priest,' the old man was unequivocal.

While the barman replenished their glasses they sat glumly in the snug to where they retired after some regular customers, renowned for their acute powers of hearing and insatiable curiosity, had established themselves. Upon receipt of the drink they took up where they had left off. This time the exchanges were conducted in whispers.

'But what can the parish priest do that a psychotherapist can't do?' Tom Collins asked.

'If word gets out that she's seeing a psychotherapist,' the old man countered irritably, 'she'll be the talk of the town and we'll never live it down. Anyway psychotherapists cost money whereas Canon Coodle will cost nothing.'

'But what does Canon Coodle know about such matters?' Tom Collins asked.

'He's a priest,' came back the incontrovertible reply. From time to time there would be silence in the public bar. The customers had reverted to their normal roles of listeners. The pair in the snug responded with a corresponding silence. When the conversation resumed on the outside a deficiency became apparent to the pair on the inside. The latter would be well aware that one of those on the outside would have been delegated by common consent to eavesdrop on those on the inside. The volume of the conversation would be raised while the eavesdropper availed himself of the best possible listening position. Often juicy titbits would be picked up especially if the occupants of the snug were less than sober, titbits that could be profitably relayed to wives and sweethearts after the pub had closed for the night.

On this occasion the eavesdropper was to be cheated. The occupiers of the snug had clammed up. After a short while they finished their drinks and left the premises. Outside they dawdled on the sidewalk before moving on to the centre of the roadway where they strolled leisurely until they had assured themselves that their voices could not carry.

'Canon Coodle it will be then,' Tom Collins agreed. 'When do you propose to see him?'

'I don't propose to see him at all,' the old man answered with a cynical laugh. 'She is your responsibility and I suggest that you see him now, right this very minute before you go to bed.'

Before Tom had time to reply he found himself being directed towards the presbytery. The old man had a firm grip on his arm and, although reluctant, Tom did not resist the pressure.

Canon Coodle listened most attentively to what his parishioner had to say. He posed no questions preferring to stimulate his caller with encouraging nods and winks. It was his experience that, by listening and by hearing the person out, all would be revealed in the end. When Tom Collins reached the end of his revelations the Canon expressed neither surprise nor dismay. He sat perfectly still for some time in case his caller might wish to add an overlooked item. When none was forthcoming he did what he always did after listening to unfortunates with puckers to resolve. He poured two large glasses of port and handed one to Tom Collins. They sipped for awhile in silence while the cleric mulled over what he had been told. He knew Tom Collins and his wife well; a model couple surely and a credit to the parish.

The cleric knew Tom's father-in-law, a domestic alarmist if ever there was one but a devout and decent man, nevertheless. The Canon wondered if he might not be at the back of his son-in-law's visit. He would not ask. He would provide instead the counsel which was expected of him. Slowly the Canon began to make up his mind and making it up he resolved that if the pucker could not be resolved by the parish with all its resources it would be a reflection on both the parish and himself.

'Before you think about seeking out expert medical advice further afield,' the Canon opened, 'you might consider exhausting the capabilities of the parish first. I mean,' the Canon continued in his homely fashion as he silently resorbed the last of his port, 'the solution to our problem could be in our own hands.'

'My father-in-law said something about sending for an exorcist,' Tom Collins suddenly put in lest he forget the matter before the conversation ended.

Canon Coodle considered the question and as he did he remembered his last meeting with Father Sylvie Mallew, the diocesan exorcist, a saintly and upright cleric who, in Canon Coodle's private estimation, would be likely to do more harm than good in this case. He had first met Father Sylvie after an unsuccessful adjuration addressed to an evil spirit which had placed an elderly lady under its power.

'Could it be,' Canon Coodle's companion of the time asked, 'that he failed to exorcise the evil spirit because there was no evil spirit to begin with?' Canon Coodle was forced to concur that this indeed might have been the case. When both clerics encountered Father Sylvie in the local hotel he was in a state of total exhaustion after the fruitless but demanding rite. The local doctor ordered him straight away to the nearest general hospital where the ailing exorcist spent a month recuperating from his ordeal. It transpired that the real evil spirit of the piece was the daughter-in-law of the old lady who had failed to come up trumps with a spirit. It was the daughter-in-law who demanded the exorcist in the first place. Later she would admit that she had been driven to it by the exorbitant demands of the old woman, by her continuous nagging and whining and by the fact that they heartily detested each other. For this and for many other valid reasons Canon Coodle was totally against calling in an exorcist especially an exorcist with the track record of Father Sylvie Mallew. He was at pains to establish his position to Tom Collins.

'You may or may not know,' he explained patiently, 'that exorcism as such is governed by the Canon Law of the Roman Catholic Church. Before consenting to an exorcism I would be bound to seek authorisation from my bishop and even then before we could get down to brass tacks it would have to be proved that we are dealing with a case of real possession. Now, you and I both know that your wife is no more possessed than you or me so let us here and now dispense with exorcism. If we don't and if we are foolish enough to resort to it your wife may very well begin to believe that she is possessed and that is almost as bad as being truly possessed.'

'What should we do then?' Tom Collins asked.

'First things first,' the Canon replied, 'so let us deal with what we know and proceed from there. You told me earlier that your wife was of the belief that she had passed herself out which is a common enough expression hereabouts. In my time I have met several people who passed themselves out to a certain degree but never to such a degree that they were not able to return to their normal selves after a certain period. I must confess,' the Canon continued warming to his task, 'that I very nearly passed myself out on a few occasions when my curates were indisposed. The fact that I did not pass myself out means that I do not take the matter seriously. Passing oneself out is really no more than an expression or at worst a flight of the imagination. From your wife's particular case we may safely draw the conclusion that she has simply looked too far ahead.'

'Years and years ahead,' her husband interrupted in an exasperated tone, 'and if she isn't stopped she'll soon be decades ahead and maybe even centuries and if that happens it is possible that she'll never return to her former self and it really means that I'll be married to a woman who isn't there at all.'

'Come, come!' the Canon resorted to one of his favourite expressions. He used it frequently when somebody forced him into a corner.

'Don't you come, come with me!' Tom Collins would never normally react in such a fashion to his parish priest but he had the feeling that the Canon was a trifle too dismissive or at the very least was not prepared to take him seriously.

'Now, now!' said the Canon.

'Don't you now, now me either!' Tom Collins turned on him. The Canon was taken completely by surprise. In every case the expressions he had used helped to mollify people, to calm them down and reassure them. The Canon was about to say 'well, well' but changed his mind in view of the agitated state of his visitor.

The Canon was now fully alerted to the fact that the time for meaningless expressions was past. He would have to approach the situation from a different angle. He would need to apply some home-made, countrified common sense.

'My wife is getting worse by the hour,' Tom Collins was on the verge of tears, 'while we sit here talking nonsense.'

'Now, now!' The expression died on the Canon's lips as he endeavoured with all his mental might to come to the aid of his parishioner. At the back of his mind's eye a picture began to form. It was a picture from the past and it was dominated by the figure of Big Bob the uncrowned king of the travelling people. It was well known to the Canon that Big Bob was not accorded regal status because of his fighting ability although he had never been beaten in a fair fight. Rather was it because of his sagacity and diplomacy although some would prefer words like roguery and guile or scheming and deception. Whatever about anybody's opinion of Big Bob he was a man of his word and once given it was never broken. Women trusted him and children followed him when he walked through the town in his swallowtail coat and Homburg hat. He was part of the community and then again he wasn't. He was a travelling man but he honoured the outskirts of the town with his presence during the winter and early spring. Then he departed, as he was fond of saying himself, for the broad road.

The picture in Canon Coodle's memory had become better developed as he tried to placate his visitor with words of
concern and understanding. The picture was still hazy and it
would remain hazy for it had happened many years before
and it had happened under moonlight so that an absolutely
clear picture was out of the question. He remembered a
woman, somewhere in her mid thirties, running in circles in
the commonage where the travelling folk were camped. It was
in that part of the commonage where the travelling folk
trained their horses so that a dirt track of almost perfect circu-
lar proportions would already be etched. A man stood at the
centre of the ring. From time to time he clapped his hands and
called out to the woman. The calls were of an encouraging
nature and the man who made the calls was none other than
Big Bob. Later when they met accidentally near the big bridge
which spanned the river the Canon's curiosity got the better of
him. He told Big Bob of what he had seen in the moonlight
and the traveller responded that the Canon had indeed seen a
woman running in a circle under the light of the moon.

'She was my sister,' Big Bob explained, 'and after her tenth
babby she lost the run of herself so I took her out to the ring
and told her to run until she caught up with herself.'

'And did she?' Canon Coodle had asked eagerly at the
time.

'Yes,' Big Bob had replied, 'she caught up with herself
soon enough and she had no more children after that.'

The Canon had been somewhat mystified but he felt as he
looked across at Tom Collins that his sudden recall of the
events in the commonage had a rare significance. By no means
a superstitious man the Canon would testify under oath that

Big Bob had no supernatural gifts but he would also testify that Big Bob was an extraordinary man with uncommon powers over his fellow travellers. It was also said of him that he had great power over horses. It was said of him too, by his detractors, that he had stolen more eggs and chickens in his heyday than any man alive but the Canon did not believe this. His fellow-travellers, especially the womenfolk, would always vindicate him on the grounds that what he stole from the well-off was stolen for hungry children and if not for hungry children then for the aged and the infirm among his clan. Then there were things he would never steal. He would never steal money and he would never steal horses. He would never steal dogs but if a dog got the notion to follow the travellers' caravans that was another story. Judges liked him. In particular district justices would listen when he made a case for a young traveller who might have been engaged in fisticuffs or window-breaking or abusive language while under the influence. Whatever the charge Big Bob would guarantee that the wrongdoer's behaviour would undergo a change for the better if he was given a chance. The travellers said of him that he kept more men out of jail than Daniel O'Connell.

The Canon was well aware that the settled community might not take too kindly to the proposal which he was about to make to Tom Collins.

'When all fruit fails we must try haws,' Canon Coodle opened. He went on to tell his visitor of what he had seen in the moonlight so many years before and of the exchanges between himself and Big Bob.

'You're not suggesting,' Tom Collins was cut off before he could finish.

116

'That is exactly what I am suggesting ...' the Canon said, 'unless, of course, you can come up with something better.'

All Tom Collins could do was shake his head. He shook it for a long while before he spoke.

'Nothing ventured, nothing gained,' he agreed resignedly.

'That's the spirit,' said Canon Coodle. 'All we have to do now is wait for a moonlit night.'

'Tonight is a moonlit night,' Tom Collins pointed out to his parish priest.

'So it is. So it is!' the Canon exclaimed joyously as he drew the curtains apart and gazed onto the gleaming lawn outside the window of his study. 'See how balmy and blessed is God's moonlight,' the Canon was quite carried away by what he saw. 'Note how it silvers the land and softens the harsher features. How blessed is the balm it brings! How sublime its serenity!' He placed a fatherly arm around the shoulders of Tom Collins who had joined him at the window. 'See where it struggles with the shadows for supremacy. How gracious is moonlight and how tranquil! See Tom where it transforms the grey of the slates on the outhouses to shining silver.'

'It's mid-winter Canon,' Tom Collins reminded the moon-struck Canon.

'So it is. So it is,' the Canon answered absently.

'Christmas is only four days away,' Tom pointed out.

'You mean,' the Canon removed his arm the better to survey the anxious face before him, 'you are contemplating doing it tonight?'

'Pray why not?' Tom asked.

'Why not indeed!' Canon Coodle agreed.

'I will go and fetch Jenny,' Tom Collins hastened towards

the door.

'And I will locate Big Bob,' the Canon announced, 'as soon as I can find my hat and coat.' After a lengthy search during which Tom Collins fretted and fumed the hat and coat were located. They left the presbytery together.

The Canon turned towards the travellers' encampment on the outskirts and the younger man turned towards the town.

'I'll see you at the entrance to the commonage,' Tom Collins called over his shoulder.

'Please God. Please God!' Canon Coodle called back.

An hour would pass before the principals in the bizarre ceremony were gathered together at the entrance to the commonage. Big Bob, replete in swallowtails, Homburg hat and flowing white silk scarf, stood with Jenny Collins at one side of the entrance while her husband and Canon Coodle stood at the other watching with undivided interest. Big Bob was speaking to the housewife. As he spoke her eyes became fixed on his. From time to time she seemed to nod her head as though she agreed with what he was saying. Not a word was borne to the watching pair although the depth and richness of the traveller's tone was clearly audible. Now and then Big Bob would raise a hand and in flowing movements would indicate the moon overhead and the myriad of stars that winked and danced in the December sky. All the time he spoke softly but all that was heard by the listeners was a purring monotone not unlike the crónáning* of a contented cat. The listeners strained but still not a word came their way. They would never know

* *Purring*

because later Jenny Collins would say that she could not recall a single word no matter how hard she tried. She would explain that she knew at the time and that things were clear to her but all had been washed away.

Finally Big Bob closed his mouth firmly and, taking Jenny Collins by the hand, led her into the commonage where they stood for awhile before he intimated with signs that she was to negotiate the circle hewn by the horses' hoofs. Big Bob took up his position in the centre of the ring and clapped his hands. At the sound of the clap Jenny Collins broke into a lively trot. She completed several circles of the ring until Big Bob called out: 'Woe, woe, woe girl!' at which she stopped. For awhile she stood silently, her eyes fixed firmly on the travelling man.

The watching pair exchanged looks of wonderment and perplexity but no word passed between them. They were aware that something extraordinary was taking place and they sensed that what was now happening was beyond words and would be threatened by external or contrary movements.

Suddenly Big Bob clapped his hands a second time at which Jenny Collins proceeded to run backwards, her steps keeping time with the clapping. As the clapping slowed so did Jenny Collins. She was now walking backwards to the slow but steady handclap, walking as though in a dream. Her husband and Canon Coodle would say afterwards when recalling the ceremony that there was a very short period when she seemed to actually float backwards although both were realistic enough to realise that it may have been some form of illusion. As the handclap slowed altogether so did the steps of the woman who had passed herself out and it became clear that instead of catching up with herself she was allowing herself to be caught up with.

'Now, now, now is the time,' Big Bob cooed.

All were agreed afterwards that cooing was the best word to describe the sound of his voice.

'Now, now, now,' he cooed again as Jenny Collins stood stock still.

'Ooh ah ooh owowow ooh ooh,' she cried out in exultation as she assumed herself back into her being.

'Extraordinary!' Canon Coodle could scarcely believe his eyes.

'Most remarkable!' he exclaimed and then, 'most peculiar entirely!'

As for Tom Collins, the poor fellow was speechless. The tears ran down his face as Jenny approached and flung herself into his waiting arms. She was his wife again, his reliable, lovable helpmate, his pride and joy, his one true love. She would never pass herself out again and she would buy her Christmas gifts like everybody else. Uncaring and oblivious to all, Jenny and Tom Collins walked through the moonlit commonage hand in hand. They would eventually arrive home but not before they had exhausted the moonlight which they would remember forever and which they found to be romantic and enchanting.

'How can we ever repay you!' Canon Coodle asked of the elderly traveller, 'may the blessings of God rain down on you like this heavenly moonlight.'

'Not by moonlight alone doth man live,' Big Bob's apocalyptic tones rose with a great ring of truth over the commonage as Canon Coodle reached for his wallet. From afar, borne upon moonbeams, came the gentle laughter of Jenny Collins.

It was the laughter of a woman who had been lost but had been found and she would remain found for every Christmas thereafter.

THE BEST
CHRISTMAS
DINNER

As Wally Pooley cycled through the countryside his faith in the goodness of his fellow humans began to waver. Wally had not eaten a bite in twenty-four hours. Hard to imagine, he thought, that the great festival of Christmas is not yet over and still there are men and women who turn the needy and the starving away from their doors.

Wally had expected the spirit of Christmas to burgeon rather than diminish as the prescribed Twelve Days slowly expired. The feast of the Epiphany, due to fall on the morrow, would see the sacred period draw to its official close and that would be that, Wally exclaimed bitterly to a fettered donkey which sought in vain for grass or vetch or any form of sustenance along the inhospitable margins of the roadway.

In many ways you and I are alike Mister Donkey, Wally concluded as he pedalled laboriously uphill; we search, often fruitlessly, for the fill of our bellies while the less worthy grow fat behind closed doors. It never occurred to him that it might be his calling that gave rise to the hostility he had experienced since setting out from his tiny house that morning. Then there was the indisputable fact that he was a townie and townies, let them be saints in their hearts, were always suspect when they ventured into the countryside.

Wally Pooley was a process server with ultimate responsibility to the minister for justice although it is doubtful if the minister in question had ever exchanged the time of day with Wally or with any other process server such was the gap that existed between the upper echelons of the ministry and the lower ranks.

Strictly speaking Wally was not obliged to serve summons until the Christmas period had passed but the pangs of hunger which had assailed him since he set out that morning might well not be assuaged until the processes were delivered and the affidavits of service signed. Then and only then would remuneration for his labours be forthcoming from the lawyers who employed him in the first place although in this instance there was only one lawyer, J. P. Holligan.

Before setting out that morning Wally had phoned his employer and acknowledged the several processes which he had received by post several days before Christmas, processes which should have been delivered immediately after their arrival but, as Wally pointed out to J. P. Holligan, he just did not have the heart to inflict so much misery on his fellow human beings with Christmas just around the corner. The truth of the matter was that Wally had been unable to rise from his lonely bed to admit the postman who would have been well acquainted with Wally's ways. When his knock failed to draw an immediate response the postman simply stood on his toes and dropped the mail through the partially opened window of Wally's bedroom. As the letters drifted downwards Wally cursed his companions of the night before, drunken wretches every one, who would not hear of his departure while he had the price of a round left in his pocket.

Wally Pooley did not rise at all that day. On the following day before departing for the public house he placed the letters carefully in the breast pocket of his shortcoat where they would remain until his last penny was spent and he would be forced to the road once more with the latest vile assortment of processes.

When he rang J. P. Holligan of Holligan, Molligan and Colligan and explained that he would need an advance so that he might purchase some simple necessities such as the fundamental bread and butter and a variety of non-luxurious items such as rashers, eggs, sausages and black puddings, the lawyer had not been in the least sympathetic, not even when it was pointed out to him that the rigours of the itinerary awaiting his humble servant would tax the energies of a professional cyclist not to mind an underfed, famished creature about to brave the elements in the pursuit of justice.

'Spare me the gruesome details,' J. P. Holligan had cut in with some vehemence. The reference to food so early in the day had added to his queasiness which had built up over the Christmas period. Undeterred, Wally Pooley laid further claim to an advance by reminding the lawyer of tricky but successful assignments in the past involving considerable physical risk and debilitating fatigue but his pleas fell on barren ground. In the end, after he had exhausted all the coins in his possession on the public phone, he had set out without bite or sup, fairly confident that a cup of tea or a plate of soup might be forthcoming from some kind soul upon his route. There were still in that part of the world some tolerant householders who made allowances for process servers even when they arrived with scripts of woe.

'Ah sure someone must do it!' the more forgiving recipients would say whilst others, not many, would make allowance by saying that it took all kinds to make a world.

The vast majority of people, rightly or wrongly, looked upon these lowly minions of the law as renegades and outcasts and would often threaten them with physical violence. The more perverted wrongdoers who would be expecting a visit from Wally Pooley would threaten him beforehand with shooting or with hanging and drowning. In his time he had been threatened with leg-breaking, head splitting, dismemberment and castration to mention but a few of the punishments to which he would be subjected should he deliver one of his processes where it wasn't wanted.

Already that morning Wally had succeeded in delivering processes for such heinous offences as property trespass by animals and humans, for debt and for assault, for breach of contract, for attempted rape and for indecent exposure. Now, as he neared the end of his hazardous itinerary, only one process remained to be served. He knew the house well. He had called there in the past but not to fulfil his legal obligations. For years before his elevation to process server he had been interested in politics and whenever canvassing parties went into the countryside in search of votes Wally went along, chiefly because he had nothing else to do but also for the good reason that the party which claimed his support was out of power and he was needed to swell the ranks of canvassers to respectable numbers.

Then, unexpectedly, after a snap election the party was returned to power and a new government was formed. Mindful of Wally's past contributions a party hack put Wally's name forward for the position of process server. Despite strong opposition because of his drinking habits and general unreliability he was duly appointed. Most of his business came from Holligan, Molligan and Colligan. The first-mentioned of these was also a government supporter and a known skinflint-cum-begrudger. The fact that he opposed the appointment of Wally Pooley worked in the latter's favour and brought him support he could not have otherwise counted upon.

The side road which led to the house where the last of the process recipients resided was seriously disfigured by potholes made doubly worse by recent rains. Wally had unhappy memories from previous visits. For one thing both the brother and sister who occupied the house were rabid supporters of the opposition and had set the farmyard dogs on Wally and his fellow-canvassers during their last visit.

As the house drew near the potholes grew larger so that Wally had the utmost difficulty negotiating them. Inevitably he was thrown from his bicycle and found himself seated in a hole full of muddy water. To add to his misfortune the three farmyard dogs appeared on the scene and proceeded to snap at him as well as bark hysterically. Quickly he rose to his feet shielding one side of his body with the bicycle and arming his free hand with a quantity of sizeable stones which he had started to gather the moment the dogs appeared. He aimed at the most savage of the three and sent him yelping to safety. The cowardly canine would continue with his intimidatory tactics while he was safely out of range. Before Wally had time to gather more ammunition the other dogs had joined the ring leader and proceeded with their criticism of the visitor from a distance.

During all this time neither of the proprietors of the great house put in an appearance. I could have been savaged to death, Wally told himself, for all they care. Shivering as he advanced along the narrow boreen he began to feel the icy cold of the water on his rear quarters. With chattering teeth he told himself aloud that he would surely fall foul of pneumonia or worse if he didn't dry himself quickly. He shook the wet trousers gingerly but all he succeeded in doing was to send the freezing drops down the backs of his thighs.

'Oh God!' he appealed in loud tones to his maker, 'what did I ever do to you that you should treat me this way?'

As he proceeded on foot the pushing of the bicycle became an almost unbearable task. Cursing and crying he longed for the sight of the house where he might heat himself for awhile by a fire. He recalled that there had been a warm range in the kitchen the last time he and his companions had managed to gain access to it. A pleasant anticipatory shudder brought him momentary relief when he remembered the glow of the fire which would shed its benign heat on him before he was much older. Even Wally's closest companions would concede that he was a poor subject for any form of hardship. Now in his forties it was certain that he had spent more of his two score years whining than celebrating. For a moment he paused and a look of alarm appeared for the first time on his face. The process! Was it still in his pocket or had he inadvertently handed it in with one of the others to the wrong recipient? His hand went instantly to his breast pocket where he kept all the letters.

He did not withdraw the safety pin. His fingers found and felt the reassuring length of the legal epistle he would shortly deliver. With a sigh of relief he proceeded.

At either side of the ancient tree-lined road, once a stately avenue, the verdant acres stretched as far as he could see, an indication of the vast wealth enjoyed by the owners, reputed to be the best-off farmers in the parish. Well off they might well be but according to locals they were so mean that even the travelling folk did not consider it worth their while to call. They left their secret signs at either side of the gate which led to the house. These signs spoke more eloquently than any conventional language of the meanness and misery of the middle-aged man and woman to whom the house and lands belonged. Another sign told of cross dogs and yet another spelt dangerous bull for it was the practice of the ungenerous pair to release one of the more dangerous bulls on to the narrow roadway in order to discourage visitors, especially travellers.

At long last the house came into view but as far as Wally Pooley could see there was no sign of a human presence. Despite the reputation of its inhabitants Wally was glad to see the thin spiral of smoke which ascended from the kitchen chimney. He looked at his watch. The noon of the day had just passed and it was at this time that country people, farmers in particular, sat down to dinner. They partook of supper in the evening after the cows had been milked or alternative stock catered for.

There were no afternoons in the countryside, only morning, evening and night. Anything after midday was looked upon as early evening. Afternoon was a word used only by landlords in former more repressive times and it had no place in the local agricultural vocabulary. It had been discarded with other words which had never fitted properly in the first place into the native ambience.

The house which stood overlooking a spacious lawn was of prepossessing proportions. It had once belonged to an English landlord whose agent disposed of it for a fraction of its value when the British pulled out after the War of Independence. The present owners were the son and daughter of the original purchaser, a man so mean that he never ate more than enough to keep him alive and who, if he had his way, would have imposed the same abstinence on those who worked for him. His offspring were somewhat different. They made certain that they always dined well themselves but, if others were to starve, surely it was not their concern.

Wally Pooley knocked tentatively at the kitchen door. It would be unthinkable, even for the owners, to use the ornate front door with its ancient elaborate knocker so stiff that it could hardly be raised, much less used. When there was no response to his knocking Wally pushed gently upon the door and was relieved when it opened easily into the warm interior. The range stood gleaming as always, a bright fire glowing in its bosom, a promising assortment of dinner utensils chortling and steaming and fragrant on its surface. He made straightaway for the range to which he immediately turned his ice-cold posterior. The warmth ran through his buttocks and then through his limbs and all his other parts while he stood entranced, utterly captivated by the exquisite heat. Such was the pleasing glow which suffused him that he could have stood thus, without moving, for hours. The steam rose behind him from the soggy seat of his trousers until the life returned to him. He would have taken off the trousers and laid them across the bars of the rack over the range but it would have been an unbecoming pose for a process server even if he had an ancient football togs underneath.

As he relaxed he drifted into a standing slumber during which he dreamed of scantily clad damsels frolicking on foreign strands. He recognised several for, after all, he had encountered them in the same place on numerous occasions in the past. They recognised him too for they contorted themselves to the most extraordinary limits in order to provoke him. One in particular took him by the hand and led him to a cave underneath towering cliffs. Inside she raised a cautionary finger to her moist lips intimating that absolute silence was required for that which was about to follow.

'Wake up you dirty devil!' The voice which exploded in his ear did not belong to any of the exotic creatures on the foreign strand. They would never address him in such a fashion. The voice belonged to Miss Clottie, the lady of the manor. Wally had some difficulty in returning to reality. When he did he found himself being glared at by Miss Clottie and her brother Master Bob.

'What are you doing here!' The decidedly unfriendly query came from Miss Clottie. Master Bob took refuge in silence knowing if there was dirty work to be done the task could not be in more capable hands than those of his beloved sister. Blurting out the words Wally explained his predicament and begged to be allowed stay a few short minutes until his trousers dried. He told them of the assault by the dogs which was a most serious matter in view of his position as a government-appointed process server. Indeed, if news of the assault

reached the ears of the proper authorities there would be hell
to pay. He was relieved to notice the look which passed between brother and sister. It was a look of mild alarm mingled
with total derision but he knew nevertheless that his words
would take heeding.

'Surely,' Miss Clottie was at it again, 'you're not trying to
tell us that you have a process for us!'

'Yes for you, you pompous oul' jade,' Wally was tempted
to reply. Instead he kept his mouth shut and awaited the same
old response which his unexpected arrival always elicited.

'The very idea,' Miss Clottie was saying, 'a process indeed
for the MacMully's of Cloontubber House! Did you ever hear
the bate of it!' She turned to her brother who had grown
strangely silent as she stood before him, hands on hips. This,
Wally Pooley told himself, is the part of the business I enjoy
the best. This job is distasteful to be sure but it has its moments
and these are they. The power of authority surged through
him. He could let them know what lay in store for them right
away by handing over the process or he could play them the
way a cat plays a mouse.

He could see, however, that while Master Bob was visibly
affected by his arrival he had made no dent whatsoever on the
uppishness of his sister. She was a snob from head to toe so she
was and wasn't it always the same with those infected by the
disease of grandeur. They believed they were so high and
mighty, so much above the ordinary, so perfect in every way
that even if there was a process in the offing nobody would
have the gall to serve it. She placed a plate of steaming soup
on the table before her brother but all he did was to stir it indif-
ferently and after awhile listlessly swallow the spoonfuls as

though they were doses of unpleasant medicine. Suddenly Miss Clottie turned on Wally Pooley, this time with arms folded.

'No Missie, no, no, no thank you,' Wally let the words run mischievously out of his mouth before she could open hers.

'No thank you for what?' she asked genuinely confused.

'For the soup you might be about to offer me.'

If she bridled under this most unacceptable jibe from a townie and a cheap townie at that she kept it to herself. She turned instead and removed the half-emptied soup plate from the table. She placed it in the kitchen sink never taking her eyes off the obnoxious creature by the range. She knew him well enough. She had seen him frequently in the town, mostly coming and going from pubs or standing in bookies' doorways when he wasn't searching for returns in bookies' windows.

'You can be on your way now,' she informed him. 'You seem to be dry enough for the road.'

'Just another minute,' he pleaded.

'Gather yourself my buck,' she threatened 'or I'll give you a second dose of the dogs.'

'Oh dear! Oh dear!' Wally Pooley addressed himself silently once more. 'They think it will never happen to them but happen it will. Processes are there to be served and they stare everybody in the face just like the hereafter. There's no escape and just because you think you're a cut above your neighbour won't excuse you. I am your local process server and like your local undertaker I will have you sooner or later.'

Wally spoke the last part aloud.

'What's he talking about?' Puzzled, she turned to her

brother for an explanation. Master Bob shrugged his shoulders while his sister's perplexity grew. Approaching the range she pushed the process server to one side and lifted one of the largest plates Wally Pooley had ever seen from the top of a pot of steaming water where she had earlier placed it so that it would be properly heated for her brother's dinner.

Intrigued, the visitor watched while she placed the items hereafter listed, on the plate; two peeled boiled potatoes, not too floury and not too soggy but precisely of the texture which had always endeared itself to the famished Wally, two medium-sized mouth-watering fillet steaks, one mound of boiled mashed parsnips, several fried onion rings, the size of small necklaces and, finally, to cover it all, a pouring of the richest, brownest gravy ever seen by Wally Pooley. Smartly she turned and placed the plate in front of her brother. She raised a hand to forestall him lest he start the course in the presence of such a lowly creature as he who had returned his bottom to the glow of the range.

'Off with you now,' she commanded.

'I'll go when my business is done,' Wally Pooley informed her.

'Then state your business now,' she demanded.

'My business is with your brother,' Wally returned.

'Then I'll go,' she said, 'but I'll be back with the dogs in fifteen minutes.'

After his sister had left Master Bob, for all his listlessness, up until that time, directed his full attention to his dinner. Wally Pooley looked on helplessly, his mouth watering, his tongue licking his lips as the head of the house lifted a forkful of choice fillet to his drooling lips. Watching him chew the juicy steak was as much as Wally could bear. Master Bob closed his eyes and raised his head the better to savour the fare. He was a slow eater. His mastications were thoughtful and deliberate. He seemed determined to extract the very last juices, the ultimate essence from everything that entered his mouth.

He should be on exhibition, Wally Pooley thought, if only to show people how much pleasure there is to be found in simple chewing. To an unobservant onlooker it might seem that he was teasing the less fortunate process server but this was not the case. Always when he masticated savoury chunks of fillet he became oblivious to all external activities. Swallowing the first forkful after what seemed, in Wally's eyes, to be an eternity Master Bob refocused his eyes on the contents of the plate. Using both knife and fork he probed and prodded and finally settled for a gravy-enriched mouthful of mashed parsnips. He held it aloft on his fork for several seconds, first cherishing and then totally admiring this contrasting titbit before slowly opening his generous mouth and lovingly depositing the parsnip therein.

There followed such a sucking and a savouring that the gathering saliva shot forth unbidden from Wally Pooley's mouth. He decided that a time for action had come and without a by-your-leave sat on a chair next to the merrily-masticating Master Bob. If the latter was aware of Wally's presence he failed to show it. He sat with his head slightly aloft, his jaws gently salivating the parsnip, his eyes closed, in a world of his own.

After the parsnip had departed to the same destination as the fillet Master Bob heaved a great sigh of satisfaction and burped appreciatively without a word of apology to the visitor. Burping secondly he reached out for a glass of milk which his sister had earlier poured for him. He swallowed noisily while the ravenous onlooker swallowed an imaginary mouthful in tandem. After the second invasion of his plate Master Bob decided the time had come for a break in the proceedings. He placed knife and fork on top of the appetising array yet to be devoured and rubbed his hands together, sighing ecstatically as he did. Then and not till then did he become aware of Wally's presence at the table. He was momentarily shocked by this outrageous breach of agricultural protocol but his annoyance slowly disappeared as he contemplated his next move.

Wally Pooley watched helplessly as the greedy eyes of his tormentor swept over the contents of the plate. Wally guessed that he would opt for an onion ring and was agreeably surprised when Master Bob decided to indulge in a second mouthful of the fillet. Carefully and lovingly he chose the section he desired, severing it neatly from the whole before impaling it on the fork prongs. Wally guessed rightly that he would wait until doomsday before Master Bob would proffer a solitary morsel from the plate where, in Wally's estimation, there was easily enough for two.

Normally Wally would not resort to the ploy which he had devised shortly before taking his place at the table but the pangs of hunger had multiplied since Master Bob had begun his meal.

Firstly he opened the safety pin which had secured his breast pocket. Secondly he withdrew the envelope which contained the process and thirdly he lifted it aloft the better to behold it and to contemplate its real value. It would also, undoubtedly, attract the attention of Master Bob but that very person was now looking out the window having risen from his seat. He gave no indication that he had noticed the envelope. He was, therefore, in Wally's opinion, relishing the food he had consumed so far. Wally had done the same thing on the rare occasions when he had been presented with high quality meals. Master Bob, he felt, would now be enjoying the interval between mastication and resumption. He would recall every bite he had eaten and would, no doubt, be considering an amalgamation of parsnip and potato or onion rings and fillet or even a medley of all four. After all, he had only barely begun and needed time to chew the cud as it were before resuming acquaintance with the constituents of his plate.

Again there was the irritating rubbing together of the hands and the even more irritating burps. When he sat again he took his implements in hand and, screwing his head this way and that, viewed his meal from every angle. The lull seemed to have sharpened his appetite for at once he uplifted a large lump of potato and parsnips, browned with an abundance of gravy.

Alas, for Master Bob, the sapid composition would never reach his mouth. A polite coughing of the best drawing-room variety was sufficient to distract him. With a perplexed look he lay the top-heavy fork on the plate. Then with a quizzical look he turned his attention to the source of the coughing. It was, indeed, his unwelcome guest the process server, the very creature he thought he had browbeaten into respectful silence. The ominous epistle was still held aloft.

'Can't it wait,' Master Bob pleaded.

'Duty calls,' came back the firm reply.

'All right, hand it over then!' There was resignation in the once haughty tone. Slowly he opened the envelope and extracted its contents. There was only one sheet of paper but on that sheet were tidings that would drain the blood from its reader's face. As he read his hands trembled and, having read, he lifted the process secondly and re-read. The second reading did nothing to restore his earlier sense of well-being.

The face was now ashen and the lips which had recently worked so feverishly and industriously were tightly drawn. Master Bob pushed his plate away and by good chance it ended nearer the hands of the process server than those of its rightful owner.

Wally Pooley's hands gently circled the plate without touching it.

'Have you finished with this?' he asked. No answer came from the sealed lips.

'You sure now!' Wally asked in a barely audible tone and yet no answer came. In that part of the world, as elsewhere, there were large numbers of people who believed that silence gives consent. Acting on this dictum Wally Pooley reached forward and seized the knife and fork which now lay idle at the head of the table. He made the sign of the Cross with the knife as he lifted the heavily-laden fork and intook its cargo so that it might be free to fulfil its role as accomplice of the knife which by now was also free to mark out a choice square of tender fillet.

As the process server stuffed himself Master Bob lifted his head in alarm from time to time. He thought he heard barking or it could have been slobbering. Another time he was convinced that he heard a pig grunting but there was no pig only Wally Pooley who was making mighty inroads into the surprise repast. As he neared the end Wally could not help but notice that Master Bob had buried his head in his hands. He availed of the opportunity to pour himself a full tumbler of milk. He wiped the plate clean at precisely the same time Miss Clottie returned with the cowardly dogs. She was shocked by what she saw at the table. She could scarcely bring herself to speak. Hurrying forward she lifted the process and started to read. In a matter of seconds her already grim visage underwent a grievous change for the worse.

Wally Pooley felt that his time for departure had come. He was already acquainted with the contents of the letter but nobody would ever hear it from him. Indeed the whole country knew that Master Bob would be contesting a paternity suit at the next sitting of the Circuit Court. Rising, as graciously as he knew how, Wally succeeded in containing the belch which would have forced its way upward and outward without apology.

'Best meal I ever ate Missie,' he directed his thanks towards Miss Clottie but that unfortunate creature was incapable of acknowledgement. Wally Pooley gently laid the knife, fork, plate and glass in the sink and backed himself out through the kitchen door, nodding his head with maximum deference as he did.

Time as only time could, would resolve Master Bob's dilemma. He would duly acknowledge the son which was undoubtedly his and he would marry the child's mother while Miss Clottie would marry a local farmer during the fall of the year and she would present her ageing husband with a son and heir nine months to the day after the knot was tied. Wally Pooley would always say that the dinner he had eaten on that eleventh of the twelve days of Christmas was the best fare ever to cross his lips. He took the full credit himself: 'For,' as he would confide to his drunken cronies many a time, 'I took my chance when it came and I delivered my process not a minute too early or a minute too late.'

THE LONG
AND THE
SHORT OF IT

LONG JASON LATTALLY WAS NOT ALONE TALL as a telephone pole but also thin as a lath, so thin, in fact, that it was a wonder he did not topple over altogether. He had a narrow jaw and he had a pointed nose and he had no lips to speak of. Consequently his eyes seemed outrageously large as did his ears and his cheek bones. People who saw him for the first time announced that he had the boniest face they ever saw. Canon Coodle, the parish priest, put it another way.

'He has a very refined face,' the Canon told his housekeeper, 'maybe a little bit too refined and we must remember that refinement is a quality sought after by many but acquired by few.'

Jason Lattally was well off by parochial standards. There was a time when he shared the family business with a brother but the poor fellow was whipped away one night by a storm as he walked along the banks of the estuary below the town. At least people presumed that he had been whipped away. In appearance there was little difference between himself and his brother Jason. If anything he was a trifle thinner and a trifle taller and a trifle hungrier-looking and maybe a trifle more lathy but for all that he was a likeable chap and when he was being transported to the graveyard on the day of his burial many notable utterances went the rounds in his favour.

Some months after his departure from the land of the living his brother Jason bought a new suit, a new shirt and a new pair of shoes and went here, there and everywhere looking for a wife. When he started out he believed that his task would be an easy one. He was now the sole proprietor of a small but successful grocery shop. The business was free of debt and contained modest living quarters as well as a back entrance which was regarded as vital to the running of a successful business in the main street of the town. Goods, for instance, might be delivered through the rear and so might fuel and it was through this rear egress that Jason exited every night to consume the few pints of stout which helped him unwind and contributed in no small way to the deep slumber which saw him wake up eager and refreshed each morning of his working week.

At first in his quest for a partner he enjoyed no luck at all. He was tempted to engage the services of a matchmaker but told himself that if he could not secure a woman through his own devices he did not deserve one. How wrong was Long Jason Lattally! Wiser men than he would testify with their hands across their hearts that a man needed all the help he could get in the isolating and securing of a suitable wife.

Time went by and at the end of a year Jason Lattally was as far from acquiring a partner as he was when he set out. Then he was informed by a female neighbour, who was aware of his plight, that there was no need for him to search afar when he might pick and choose from the selection under his very nose. He had many female customers who were of the marrying age and, more importantly, of the marrying bent.

When Madame Lucia Palugi the famous Dublin fortune teller came to town and set up shop for a week in the front room of a small house, several doors down the street from the premises of Long Jason Lattally, Jason decided to pay her a visit. She was a somewhat obese lady of indeterminate age but she had earned for herself an unrivalled reputation as a clair-voyant. After she had carefully read Jason Lattally's palm she informed him that he had a lifeline which suggested that he would reach the ripe old age of one hundred and two. She also informed him that he was unmarried and when he asked her how she could tell she merely pointed at the crystal ball which dominated the top of the table at which they sat. Peer though he did with all his might, Jason saw nothing in the crystal. The opposite was the case with the noted prophetess. She saw two women, one tall, thin and rangy and the other short and stocky. Jason Lattally informed her with mounting astonish-ment that he knew both women, that both were in fact, regu-lar customers of his although he had never seriously contem-plated either.

'That may be,' he was told amiably and Madame Palugi went on to tell him that while he might not be enamoured of them they were most certainly enamoured of him, 'and,' she continued without a tremor in her tone, 'one or other of the pair will be the mistress of your abode before Christmas for I see before me in my crystal ball a pair of legs which are defi-nitely not yours and these legs happen to be in position under your kitchen table. I cannot say whether the legs are long or short and I cannot see a trace of a face because my crystal is somewhat clouded but it is a fact that the owner of the legs will be your wife before Christmas.'

Madame Palugi had seen nothing in her crystal ball but she was well informed nevertheless. The lady who owned the house where Madame Palugi foretold the future had filled her in as soon as Long Jason Lattally entered and, as he sat in the tiny ante-room awaiting his turn to be divined, much was revealed about his background and romantic aspirations. At the end of the session he was prepared to accept the fact that he would have a wife before Christmas and that she would be one of the two women mentioned by the fortune teller. He decided after a sleepless night that his future wife would be the tall, thin woman and not the short, stocky one. The tall, thin candidate, by name Alicia Mullally, was less plain than the stocky candidate and besides that she was possessed of a considerable fortune, had already acquired some business acumen and had the reputation of being an excellent housekeeper.

The shorter woman whose name was Elsie Bawnie could fairly be described as being sober and industrious and had plenty too by way of worldly goods. She had a certain charm and came from a family renowned for its honesty although in that particular place at that particular time people hid their money and stowed away their valuables at the mere mention of the word honesty.

'I have never met an honest man with the exception of Canon Coodle,' Big Bob the Traveller was fond of saying, 'and I'm pretty sure that I never will. Even if a man is honest,' Big Bob would continue, 'he has already given a hostage to fortune because of his physical attachments and may not be trusted altogether.'

When Jason Lattally approached Alicia Mullally as she left the local greengrocers with a packet of birdseed she was quite taken aback and did not know whether to laugh or cry. She leaned her long frame forward like a heron about to snatch a sprat and would have flapped homewards straight off had not Jason seized her gently by the sleeve of her calico blouse and restrained her.

'Will you?' he asked.

'Will I what?' she responded as though she had not heard the first time.

'Will you marry me?'

When she remained tightlipped he repeated the question and still she would not commit herself. It was not the first time that such a question had been put to Alicia Mullally. She had always answered in the negative in the past and had regretted her decision at least twice. At the time she had convinced herself that they would ask again and indeed they had asked again but not Alicia. What a strange place, she told herself, for a man to propose and was it, she asked herself, an indication of other strangenesses? Strangenesses were the last thing she wanted. Like all women she wanted a man she could depend on. She did not, however, say no. She tried to draw away but she did not try very hard. He still held her firmly by the sleeve.

'Will you or won't you?' he said and she deduced that if the answer was not in the affirmative there might not be a second offer. Their eyes met and she could see that he was deadly serious. He had paled almost beyond recognition and she guessed that he had built up his courage for some time before approaching her. When she spoke again her voice had softened and there was sympathy in her eyes. She laid a hand on the hand that held her by the sleeve.

'Why don't you call to the house sometime?' she whispered invitingly. 'This is no place to talk about marriage.'

Jason Lattally released his hold and assured her that she could expect him that very night when he would be hoping for a positive answer.

News of the proposal spread quickly. In the space of one hour the whole street was fully informed. In the space of two the town knew that Long Jason Lattally would be calling to the abode of Alicia Mullally that very night. It was believed that she would accept but not before she hummed and hawed her fill. She was of the breed of hummers and hawers and breeding will out.

'You will find breeding in turnips,' Big Bob the Travelling Man would say. 'Why man,' he would continue in his homely way, 'you will find breeding in the poll of a hatchet, in the handle of a scythe, in the straw of your thatch, in the spokes of your wagon.' He would go on and on until his audience drifted away.

The first thing Big Bob did when he heard of the proposal was to trim his flowing white mohal.* The second thing he did was to visit his friend Bertie Bawnie, the father of the town's smallest woman but not so small as not to be marriageable. It was Elsie herself who opened the door.

'Small yes!' Big Bob silently said to himself, 'but ugly no.'

* *Abundant fleecy hair.*

145

The travelling man was greeted warmly. It would not be in her breeding to do otherwise. Big Bob recalled her late mother who had been renowned for her generosity and courtesy. It was, therefore, inbred into Elsie. She ushered him through the small pork shop to an even smaller kitchen where her father sat snoozing by a bright peat fire. Bertie Bawnie had a round pink face atop a small chunky body. He rose at once to his feet when he saw who his visitor was. Expansively he indicated a chair and with a well rehearsed motion of wrists and fingers indicated to his daughter that she was to fetch glasses and whiskey. Not until a glass of whiskey had been consumed in the most leisurely fashion by each of the elders was a word spoken.

'What brings you friend?' Bertie Bawnie asked as he replenished both glasses.

'I have come matchmaking,' came the solemn reply. The traveller was quick to elaborate.

'It has come to my attention,' he said, 'that Long Jason Lattally is about to propose to Alicia Mullally and it has further come to my attention,' he went on, 'that the daughter of this house would be far better suited to Lattally but I need that daughter's permission and I need her father's permission before I can make a case.'

An uncomfortable silence greeted the traveller's announcement. Big Bob had made a match or two in the past but mostly among the travelling people. If the truth were told he would be more of a consultant than a matchmaker. He would be fully versed in the lore of the countryside and would be aware of the failings and virtues of marriageable men and women along the roads which he travelled regularly. He would be cognisant of the background and breeding of likely partners and he always made himself available whenever vital information was required by professional matchmakers. He had a priceless stock of valuable knowledge and he was easy to deal with as far as consultancy fees were concerned.

The Bawnies, father and daughter, replied to his proposal in their individual ways and in their own time; the daughter by refilling the glasses as soon as they were drained and the father by asking if Big Bob would be interested in acting on his daughter's behalf. A considerable amount of whiskey was consumed before the deliberations came to an end. The chief worry entertained by Bertie Bawnie was that Long Jason Lattally might have already proposed.

'I think not,' Big Bob reassured him, 'for it has come to my attention that Alicia Mullally is a dawdler who finds it difficult to make up her mind. She should and could have been married years ago but she kept putting the matter on the long finger.'

Bertie Bawnie countered by saying that it was his belief there would be a Mullally/Lattally marriage before Christmas and that Christmas was almost down on the door.

'You may have made your move too late,' he concluded unhappily.

'Not so,' Big Bob answered. 'Now is the time to make the move for it has come to my attention that Long Jason is due to propose at nine o'clock tonight.'

'It is now eight.' Elsie Bawnie spoke for the first time and it occurred to Big Bob that she had the demurest way and the most subtle way of making a point.

'I'll go now,' he said in dramatic tones, 'and I'll state my case to Long Jason Lattally.'

Elsie followed him to the door and, taking him by the hand, thrust a ten pound note therein.

'There will be ninety more,' she promised, 'if you succeed in your mission for if I can't have Long Jason I won't have anybody. He is all that's left of the Lattallys and I am all that's left of the Bawnies, barring my Da.'

As he drew his coat about him preparatory to crossing the street for his proposed confrontation with Long Jason, Big Bob was forestalled by the distant but resonant tones of the last remaining male Bawnie.

'There's another hundred from me,' the voice said, 'if the news is joyful.'

There was no question but that the Bawnies had great faith in the travelling man. There were few others who were possessed of the same faith and, surprisingly, one of these was Canon Coodle although it would have to be said that his faith was limited. Still faith was faith regardless of its consistency. Big Bob was fully aware that father and daughter trusted him fully and he was quite moved as a result. The expression 'faith can move mountains' was familiar to him. He had heard it often enough in church and had come to set great store by the ancient proverb. There had been an occasion of celebration around the campfire when the travellers would philosophise at length about religion and about the world at large. The happy group had just run out of liquor and the tragedy was that the combined finances of the travellers was not sufficient to purchase a single bottle of stout. Big Bob had volunteered to approach one of the town's public houses where he would request credit.

While most of the publicans did not encourage the travelling folk to drink on their premises there were occasions when they could be depended upon to extend a small amount of credit. He had been a young man then and his listeners had scoffed at the very thought of his demanding credit from a publican.

'Oh ye of little faith,' he said at the time whereupon a rival responded that travellers could not be expected to have as much faith as settled people as past experiences would show.

'The Good Book tells us that faith can move mountains,' Big Bob countered, 'and it don't say what kind of faith so it seems to me that my faith is good enough for this kind of task.' The credit had been forthcoming but Big Bob could never be sure whether it was his faith or the fact that the publican was drunk at the time.

Now as he knocked on Long Jason Lattally's door he prayed for resolve. When he beheld his caller Long Jason presumed that the traveller had come a-begging. He thrust his hand into his trousers pocket and handed over a silver coin. The traveller accepted the money and expressed his gratitude but explained that he had not come seeking alms.

'I believe,' Big Bob said, 'that you intend getting married.'

Long Jason Lattally laughed. 'And what has that got to do with you?' he asked.

'If you'll be good enough to let me in I'll tell you everything,' Big Bob promised.

The long man consulted his watch and, seeing that he had the best part of an hour to spare, stepped to one side so that his caller might enter. Inside they both sat but there was no drink on view.

'Will whiskey be all right?' the long man asked, his bare-boned face breaking into a smile.

'Whiskey is just what I need.' Big Bob moistened his lips.

Long Jason filled two glasses. Normally he drank only in a public house and always illegally after hours since he was of the belief like many of his neighbours that drink taken at home involved no risk and, therefore, lost much of its potency. He had on this occasion, decided to make an exception on the grounds that he needed some sort of booster if he was to successfully propose to Alicia Mullally. Both men sipped their drinks for awhile and exchanged well worn items of news.

'So!' Long Jason Lattally stretched his legs and awaited the pronouncement that would justify his visitor's intrusion.

'So!' came back the long, drawn-out response. Big Bob rose to his feet and placed his hands behind his back. 'I have come,' he said solemnly, 'to ask if you would consent to a life-long traipse with Elsie Bawnie?'

'A life-long traipse eh!' Long Jason pondered the phrase. He had not heard it before and felt that it was not a bad description at all of the undertaking implied.

'And by whose authority do you present yourself here with such a proposal?' he asked.

'By the girl herself with the full approval of her father,' Big Bob answered.

'I had an inkling that she was that way inclined.' Long Jason pulled upon his jaw until Big Bob felt that he might pull it off altogether, so thin and finely pointed was it.

'It's like the bottom end of a sickle moon,' Big Bob thought. 'Are you interested?' he asked as he resumed his seat.

'She's small,' the long man replied, 'and she's nice, danged nice but with me being so tall and she being so small we'd be a laughing stock.'

'For a short while only,' Big Bob assured him, 'and then only when the pair of you would be upright. You will never meet such a lady for charm, a lady that so knows her place. She would make a man happy and she would bear the finest of children.'

'I know, I know,' the long man found it difficult to contain his irritation, 'but the bother is that I have more or less contracted to propose to Alicia Mullally. In fact she awaits me this very night.'

'If you have any sense,' Big Bob spoke forcibly, 'you'll let her wait.'

'I can't do that,' said the long man.

'Those who have awaited,' Big Bob informed him solemnly, 'have been elated and those who have gone have been put upon.'

'What's that from?' Long Jason asked anxiously.

'That is from the book of travellers,' came the reply, 'verse one, chapter two.'

'Elsie Bawnie is a very small woman and I am a very tall man,' Long Jason was adamant.

'And what of Alicia Mullally?' Big Bob asked. 'Are not the pair of ye too tall for your own good and whoever heard of an equal pairing making a good match. For a true marriage,' Big Bob went on, 'you need opposites, the fair and the dark, the stout and the skinny, the stooped and the straight, the tall and the small. This tall dame could be the very death of you my poor man. She is not suited to you at all.'

Long Jason was impressed in spite of himself but he was

determined to fulfil his tryst.

'Tonight,' he clenched his fists as he spoke, 'I embark on the most important mission of my life to date. Tonight I will open my heart to the woman who will one day be the mother of my children and I plan to have many. I would not be alone now if my mother had brought more children into the world so you see it's important that I get started without any more delay.'

'I was never a man,' Big Bob looked into the fire, 'to pour cold water on the plans of a lover but you could be starting on the road to ruin and I cannot in all conscience stand idly by while you destroy yourself.'

'What do you mean?' Long Jason grew more apprehensive with every passing moment.

'Did you ever ask yourself where is the windiest spot in the country?' Big Bob was master of the situation now. This was his field. He belonged where he was and he would make the most of it.

'The windiest spot in the country!' Long Jason was puzzled. He decided nevertheless to answer the question. 'They say,' he replied, 'that the right bank of the estuary about a mile below the bridge is the windiest spot of all.'

'Windy enough to blow the hair off a man's head?' Big Bob asked.

'Windier,' came back the instant response.

'Windy enough to blow a man's false teeth back his throat and out you know where?'

'Windier,' came the emphatic reply.

'Windy enough to blow a man away altogether?'

'Yes,' came the answer, 'and who knows it better than my

poor self that lost his only brother in a south-west gale and he out walking for the good of his health.' Long Jason shook his narrow head in sorrow. The tears rolled down without hindrance because of the shape of his face. They fell on his freshly-shone shoes and they fell on the floor and as he continued to shake his head they fell with a hiss and a fizz into the kitchen fire. When he had cried his fill he lifted the whiskey bottle and recharged the glasses. Before he raised his drink to his lips he olagóned* his fill. It is the nature of this man to olagón, Big Bob told himself, and there is no point in asking him to desist for all his ancestors were olagóners and keeners and would raise their voices in the most melancholy fashion at the slightest opportunity. Eventually the olagóning came to an end and Long Jason raised his glass to the memory of his dead brother. Big Bob raised his and drained his and said what a pity it was that such a man should be swept away especially when he need not have been swept away at all.

'How's that?' Long Jason asked.

'How's what?' Big Bob returned innocently.

'You said that he need not have been swept away at all.'

'Did I?' Big Bob's voice was filled with surprise. 'Ah yes,' he reflected, 'so I did, so I did.'

'Explain.' Long Jason's request fell on receptive ears.

'What restrains the ship when the storm blows and the wind howls? Think before you answer.' Big Bob was on a familiar tack.

'Why the anchor restrains the ship,' Long Jason replied.

* *Cry, lament*

'And who is the last to yield in the tug-of-war?' Big Bob asked as he raised the back of his coat and toasted his posterior to the fire.

'Why the anchor man of course,' Long Jason replied. It was clear that he was beginning to enjoy the questions and answers exercise, especially since he found no difficulty in answering. He awaited the next poser with confidence.

'What was your brother anchored to when he was blown away?' Big Bob asked.

'Why he was anchored to nothing,' came the response.

'And if he was anchored to something do you think he would be blown away?'

'It would have to be something mighty solid,' the long man replied.

'Mighty solid,' Big Bob paced the kitchen raising his empty glass and placing it on the mantelpiece over the fire. 'And do you think, for instance, if he had a long thin dame the likes of Alicia Mullally by his side that she would be solid enough to anchor him against the force of the wind?'

'She most certainly would not,' came the scornful response.

'Isn't it likely,' Big Bob was now standing in the centre of the kitchen, his hands joined like an advocate 'isn't it likely,' he reiterated, 'that instead of your brother being blown away on his own that his companion would be blown away as well?'

'I don't have any doubt whatsoever about it,' Long Jason affirmed. 'In fact,' he concluded, 'any man who would go walking with such a female on the right hand bank of the estuary should have his head examined.'

'Would you go walking with such a woman on the afore-

mentioned spot?' Big Bob looked up the chimney from the ex-
pansive hearth. He noticed that it badly needed cleaning. He
wasn't a sweep himself but he was not above holding a ladder
for a modest fee.

'I certainly would not walk with her on the right hand
bank of the estuary.'

'There are other windy places,' Big Bob pressed on with
his advantage, 'and no matter where you are you cannot write
off the unexpected squall. Any time you walk with a dame as
long and as thin and as light and as frail and as unsteady as
Alicia Mullally you are putting your life at risk. Now let us
suppose that you are out walking with Elsie Bawnie and that
suddenly the wind rises and you find yourselves on the right
hand bank of the estuary with no shelter and nowhere to turn.
What would you do? I'll tell you what you would do. You
would hold on to Elsie Bawnie for there is no squall and there
is no wind and there is no storm that would blow her away.
The heavens have yet to invent a gale that would bowl her
over. I defy the blasts and the gusts that sweep in from the
foaming sea. Let them rage and roar but they won't budge
Elsie Bawnie one inch and I'll lay my hat and cloak on that and
my old black mare plaited and ribboned and my painted car-
avan. I can see it all now in my mind's eye. I can see yourself
and the long woman leaning into one another against the force
of the storm and finding no purchase in yeerselves or anywhere else, here one minute and gone the next, gone and
swept and carried forever in the belly of the blast, out past the
headland and across the roaring sea to lands unknown, never
to be seen again and may God in his mercy forgive you your
sins in the name of the father, the son and the holy ghost. Then

I see you in another calamity and the wind about to lift you like a paper kite when all of a sudden who comes along, who comes along I ask you? Come on man and answer me. Who comes along?'

'Elsie Bawnie comes along,' Long Jason Lattally roars aloud as though he were imbued by the spirit of the sou' wester.

'She takes your hands.'

'She takes my hands.'

'She holds you down.'

'She holds me down.'

'She wraps her arms around your legs.'

'She wraps her arms around my legs.'

'She leads you home to safety.'

'She leads me home to safety.'

'To your warm bed where she lies you down.'

'To my warm bed where she lies me down.'

'And ministers into you with all her holy powers.'

'And ministers into me with all her holy powers.'

'Forever and ever amen.'

'Forever and ever amen.'

Jason Lattally raised his long bony arms aloft 'forever and ever' he called out and pushing his mentor to one side dashed through the door and did not draw breath until he found himself with the same long, bony arms around Elsie Bawnie to whom he proposed when he regained his breath and by whom he was accepted.

Big Bob, somewhat exhausted from his intercessory endeavours, laid hands on the bottle of whiskey which stood invitingly on the kitchen table. He raised it to his lips and swallowed long and swallowed hard until some of his strength returned. Then he sat and planned. There is much to be done, he told himself, and there is much coin to be made if I play my cards right and before this night is down I'll turn the trump in my favour not once but many times. He allowed himself another quarter hour of leisurely drinking before combing his mohal* and re-arranging his apparel.

Five minutes later he stood in the kitchen of the abode of Alicia Mullally. She was surprised to see him. She had been expecting another person entirely she told him.

'I have come,' Big Bob spoke with all the authority he could muster, 'on behalf of Bertie Bawnie, a man who loves you dearly, a man who will cater to all your needs and place his monies at your disposal and, although he is of small stature, were he to stand on top of his money he would be the tallest man in this town.' Big Bob went on as he had with Long Jason Lattally pointing out the danger from gales and squalls that lurked everywhere awaiting long thin victims. When he had finished Alicia Mullally begged him to convey her love to the smallest man in the town, the anchor of anchors, Bertie Bawnie.

Giddy with the promise of another hundred pounds Big Bob arrived at the abode of Bertie Bawnie. The poor fellow sat by the fire caterwauling as no cat ever could while he lamented the imminent departure of his daughter who had just agreed to be the wife of Long Jason Lattally before the advent of Christmas.

* *Abundant fleecy hair*

Big Bob drew up a chair and stretched his legs towards the fire. Slowly and melodiously for such was the timbre of his rich voice, he pointed out the benefits of attaching oneself to a woman with the length and suppleness of Alicia Mullally, with the leanness of her and the keenness of her and the slender yielding frame of her. He was at his most poetic when he described the pair as he envisaged them walking along the right bank of the estuary. Overhead the wild geese flew in stately skeins to their feeding grounds while seabirds of every denomination mewed and bleated. He saw them walk hand in hand towards a setting sun and suddenly from the south-west came great black stormclouds and in a matter of seconds all hell broke loose. Everything that was unattached was blown away, everything except Bertie Bawnie, and just as Alicia was about to be whipped away to God knows where by the all-conquering winds of the west she was seized around the midriff by her stocky partner and saved from a watery grave. He went on and on, inventing countless perilous situations where always the stocky partner was at hand when an anchor was needed.

After a full hour of Big Bob's blather Bertie Bawnie was on his knees imploring the king of the travellers to make a case for him. When Big Bob declared that the case had been successfully made Bawnie danced on the kitchen table and jumped like a stag over every chair in the kitchen which was no small feat when one took his size into consideration. He willingly paid over the promised hundred for the successful pairing of Long Jason Lattally and his daughter Elsie plus another hundred for his negotiating the not-too-distant Christmas nuptials of Bertie himself and the overjoyed Alicia Mullally.

As Big Bob wended his unsteady way homewards the first flakes of snow alighted on his broad shoulders. It had been a great night's work entirely and to think that he might never have contemplated embarking on a matchmaking venture at all but for the fact that his old friend, the saintly Canon Coodle, had complained to him in the late autumn that the population of the parish was declining and that unless there was an increase in the number of marriages there was a danger that it would decline further.

'I haven't presided over a christening in three solid weeks,' Canon Coodle said sadly, 'and from latest intelligence reports I have deduced that it will be at least another three before there's any change.'

Canon Coodle always looked upon his housekeeper and sacristan as the intelligence officers of the parish and he knew from experience that their sources were impeccable.

Big Bob would never let the Canon know about his efforts on the elderly clergyman's behalf. Was not virtue its own reward and was he not several hundred pounds better off than when he had set out that evening! He raised his great head to sniff the snow-laden wind and thanked his maker for his successes on the matchmaking front. Surely in a short while the cries of infants would be heard once more in the parish but first would come the bells of marriage and then, after consummation, the merry bells of Christmas.

CHRISTMAS ERUPTIONS

THERE ARE MORE ROWS AT CHRISTMAS THAN any other time of year but they are rows of shorter duration even if they are rows of greater intensity. Then, of course, I am a man who supports the theory that there can be no true happiness in any household without a flaming eruption now and again.

I am not talking about the joy that comes with the making-up which is fine in itself. Rather am I talking about the dispelling of those noxious gases which gather over long periods of calm and lassitude. I refer too, of course, to subjugated feelings and dispositions which have turned evil over the course of time as well as all the other ups and downs which assail the human make-up. If these are not unleashed and if they are retained unnecessarily the human spirit will corrode and instead of relationships which are vibrant and vital there will be inevitable stagnation and you will never have the air-clearing, heart-warming confrontations necessary to the successful maintenance of the human system.

People tend to behave too properly at Christmas and where this happens an outbreak of one kind or another is inevitable. Too-proper behaviour is not natural in that it suppresses the mischief and blackguardism inherent in all of us, barring a sainted few.

If this natural mischief is not vented at regular intervals there can only be two consequences, i.e., stagnation or violence and bad as the latter is the former is even worse because a stagnant home is no home and a stagnant marriage is God's greatest curse. The occasional verbal outbreak, therefore, is a vital ingredient in the successful marriage.

The most dangerous of the Christmas denizens is the common or garden senior male of the household. Nearly always he is likely to be a chap who is set in his ways and who may like to lie down quietly after the excesses of Christmas Day. The best treatment for this type of Yuletide invalid is to guide him to a secluded room and to place a Do-Not-Disturb sign on the door.

If he is suddenly awakened by some accidental intrusion it should be considered a wise manoeuvre to vacate the vicinity of the room where he rests.

Other dangerous denizens are senior married females who have been pushed too far all day and taken for granted over too long a time. The bother here is that outbreaks are totally unpredictable because females tend to suffer silently and give little indication of the explosive scenes which can and do occur as a matter of course in every respectable household.

When these suppressed housewives erupt it is always wise for outsiders to make for the nearest exit until the cataclysm subsides.

Thankfully Yuletide outbreaks, whether male or female, tend to be of short duration. They should be encouraged up to a certain point, however, for the good of the persons in question and for the good of the family as a whole. One of the most devastating Christmas rows ever to occur in the street where I was born happened a short while before the Christmas dinner. We shall call them Tom and Mary.

Tom was sitting by the fire sipping from a glass of whiskey. Mary was sipping from a glass of sherry as was the wont with females at that time.

'Will you have peas or beans with your turkey?' Mary asked politely.

'It's immaterial to me,' Tom responded with equal civility.

'Make up your mind now like a good man for I haven't all day,' said Mary who had been on the go since daybreak attending to the myriad chores which needed her attention.

'I really don't care one way or the other,' Tom persisted.

'Dammit!' said Mary peevishly, 'will you make up your bloody mind,' whereat Tom told her what she could do with the peas and beans whereat Mary informed him that he was a thankless wretch whereat Tom smashed his glass against the floor whereat they harangued each other without mercy and without let-up for a quarter of an hour whereat they both grew exhausted and fell into each others arms whereat all was peaceful again and instead of having peas or beans they had both peas and beans together and a happy Christmas to boot.

A LAST CHRISTMAS GIFT

THE TWINS WALLY AND CARL HERN BORE not the slightest resemblance to each other. Wally was several inches taller and several stones heavier.

From the day they could walk Wally was as easygoing as Carl was mettlesome. Wally's features were uniform and softly drawn against Carl's angled, almost severe lineaments.

Carl's nose was unusually long and pointed, his jaw jutting and hooked, contrasting sharply with Wally's chubbiness.

Wally's was a slow, lumbering gait whereas Carl's was precise and undeviating. Wally was a careless dresser. Carl was natty and orderly.

In temperament the difference between the pair was more marked. Wally was an amiable hunk of boyhood slow to rouse, easy to mollify.

Carl, on the other hand, angered easily, was ever alert for slights and took offence from seemingly innocuous banter. When this happened redress was immediate and painful. He was clever with his fists. Add to this the looming form of his twin brother continually dominating the background and it was easy to understand why he never lost a fight.

From an early age Carl was to grow more and more perplexed by his brother's cheerful disposition, his way with people, old and young alike, the ease with which he shrugged off affronts and other forms of disparagement which seemed intolerable to Carl. Inevitably the perplexity turned to resentment and eventually to jealousy but this was not to fully fester for some time. It would remain dormant for a period thanks to the intervention and shrewd good sense of the twins' mother Maisie.

There were five other children but the twins were the eldest. In their tenth year their father lost himself in the East End of London where it was said he had settled in with another woman. Maisie Hern made no attempt to locate her husband. She sent no word reminding him where his real responsibilities lay. She was too proud for that. Anyway where was the satisfaction in holding a man against his will! She simply readjusted herself and made the most of the situation.

She was quick to interpret the dark scowls and barely-subdued mutterings of the smaller twin whenever Wally came in for any sort of favourable mention from neighbours or others. It was the concealed menace underneath Carl's surface discontent that worried her. He became more snarly and vituperative at each recital of his brother's accomplishments.

One night his spleen erupted into a vicious physical assault. A furious fight followed. Maisie Hern, shocked, sat powerless until it ended. At first it seemed that the bigger, stronger Wally must yield to the passionate yet accurate onslaughts of the smaller twin. He took a severe pummelling in the early stages and was content to merely defend himself. He was, in fact, unable to do anything more. Then as Carl's fury slowly abated after the first murderous offensives the superior strength of the bigger twin asserted itself.

Carl clung to his brother for dear life knowing that if he let go he would be knocked senseless. Inexorably Wally forced him to arm's length and drew back his clenched fist preparatory to delivering a stunning chastisement. Slowly, however, he managed to gain control of himself. His whole body slackened as did his grip on Carl. He opened his fist and looked at his hand in puzzlement, wondering how it had ever come to be closed in the first place.

Seizing his opportunity Carl made a last do-or-die attack but there was no strength left in him. He spent himself fully and futilely until he was forced to hold on to the table for support. Wally wiped his own face clean of blood and handed the cloth to Carl. Unperturbed Wally went upstairs to bed.

Word of the fight spread. Maisie Hern had to confide in somebody and who better than a neighbour especially since her husband had deserted her. Maisie had fully recognised the value of the fight. It had shown her that Wally could contain Carl without physical domination. The neighbour suggested boxing gloves and undertook to instruct the boys in their use.

The twins were to fight many times after that first occasion but never privately. Encouraged by Maisie they were much sought after by pubs and clubs. Whenever there was a boxing tournament anywhere near they occupied a special place on the bill. Wally never won or never seemed to win but he did not mind that. There was always a bag of sweets or fruit after the fight. Deep down he knew that he must let Carl have his way. It was the only means of keeping his brother's insane jealousy on a leash.

Without the mollification of these public victories there was no telling what form the smaller twin's jealousy might take. The fights always followed a fixed pattern. Unlike the first conflict in the kitchen it was Wally who had the better of matters in the early stages of all the fights thereafter. He would, of course, be roundly booed by the crowd. After all he was nearly twice the size of his seemingly gamier, pluckier opponent. Acting to the prescribed pattern, Carl would feign hurt and injury as he allowed himself to be thumped and slapped around the ring. He was not above taking a count at times while the onlookers shouted themselves hoarse for his recovery.

At the end of the first one-and-a-half-minute round those who were unacquainted with the procedure would call upon the referee to discontinue the bout. The second round was but a repetition of the first with Carl at the time at the receiving end of what seemed to be countless, callously-delivered punches. Midway through the third and final round he would bring the crowd to its toes with an all-out, unexpected assault on Wally.

He would throw punches from every conceivable angle. There were flurries and combinations bewildering to behold. As the bigger twin wilted under the sustained barrage there was hysteria all around. When he finally fell to the canvas, unable to rise, the crowd went berserk. Carl beamed, when after the count, his hand was raised aloft. The blows had been real enough even if they had little or no effect on Wally. He lay there patiently until a second lifted him to his corner. He fully realised that as long as Carl was chalking up such victories there was an assurance of peace in the home. He was well content to play the role of underdog. He was worried by the fact that sooner or later they would outgrow this form of confrontation. He hoped with all his heart that such a day might never come. He hoped in vain.

Time passed and with puberty came the realisation that the fighting must end. Anyway they had ceased to be a draw. This sort of bout was strictly for children and children they no longer were. Despite her circumstances Maisie contrived to send them to secondary school. For the first few months all went well until both boys sat for a house examination. Unfortunately, Wally secured better marks. Neither did particularly well but the fact that Wally had shown himself to be the better of the two brought a return of the old anxiety to himself and his mother. They had not long to wait. Carl absented himself from school the very day after the results were made known. Every so often after that he would spend a day touring the countryside while Wally invented different excuses to cover his absence.

Came the next house examination and the positions were reversed. Wally had seen to that. Both boys fared poorly, so poorly that the president of the school, Father Ambrose, suggested to Maisie that it might be a more sensible course if the boys were apprenticed to trades. Being a deserted wife Maisie occupied the same status as a widow and as such had little difficulty in persuading two local tradesmen to take the boys on.

Carl was apprenticed to a plumber and Wally to a carpenter. In a short while Wally was making himself useful around the house. He showed an aptitude for woodwork from the beginning and although Carl was adapting himself without difficulty he was presented with no opportunity to display his developing skills. Inevitably the jealousy crept in. Wally wisely desisted from any further enhancement of the home. From that time onward he never even mentioned his work.

Eventually both boys completed their apprenticeships and were retained in employment by their masters. Then came the incident of the greyhound. Wally's master, in his spare time, was a respected breeder of coursing dogs and like all such devotees was forever seeking likely converts to the sport. Wally seemed to him to be an ideal candidate. He, therefore, presented him free of charge with a black greyhound pup on the final day of his apprenticeship.

Carl, not to be outdone, with the accumulated wages of several weeks, went further afield and purchased a white pup of impeccable background from another breeder.

Carl's was clearly the better prospect for a distinguished coursing career. He was perfectly bred and shaped exceptionally well as a sapling. Wally's charge clearly lacked the style and class that were so evident from the outset in his brother's hound.

Then came the annual coursing meet when both dogs were entered for a stake confined to no-course duffers. Carl's dog started as a clear favourite and at the end of the day had effortlessly won his way to the final. Wally's also managed to scrape his way to the final course but was given no chance against his better-bred, lightly-raced opponent.

It was at this juncture that Wally's master stepped in. An old hand at the doing-up of tired finalists he took charge of the unfancied black. He set to work on the dog's back and shoulders with his powerful hands until the exhausted hound responded and started to show signs of gameness. From his hip pocket he extracted a flask of poitín and applied the stimulating liquid to the dog's pads. He poured a dram into his palm and forced it into the dog's mouth. After some initial spluttering the creature shook its head and pricked its ears, declaring its gameness for the coming course.

On his master's advice Wally refused the first three calls to slips and it was only when threatened with disqualification that he deigned to lead his dog to the start. Carl's white was meanwhile left to fret and whimper in anticipation of the hare's breaking. The longer he was kept at the slips the more would be taken out of him for the rigorous buckle that lay ahead. It was an old trick, frequently resorted to by handlers whose hounds needed time to recover their strength.

The slip was a fair one. The black carried the white collar, the white the red. From the moment they were slipped the pair were inseparable. The hare was a strong and stagy one and had been especially held over for the ultimate buckle. With half the course covered they had come within a length of the fleeing puss. The white hound seemed to forge ahead but then with a tremendous surge the black excelled himself and put his nose to the fore. He lifted the unfortunate hare effortlessly in powerful, murderous jaws. In a second the creature was being cruelly torn apart between the two dogs. The black had won. He had killed in his stride in text-book manner. If the dark look that over-shadowed Carl's taut face spelt extreme disappointment the look of alarm that crossed Wally's spelt disaster. He was, therefore, mightily relieved when Carl congratulated him on the win. It was only a temporary respite. He knew no good would come of his success and cursed himself for allowing his master to take charge of the handling.

In the morning when Wally went to the makeshift kennel to take the black for his morning exercise the hound lay stretched in a pool of blood, its throat cut. Without a word to anybody he located an old coal sack in which he deposited the bloodied carcass. He heaved it on to his back and made his way circuitously to one of the deeper holes in the nearby river, making certain that he was seen by nobody. On the river bank he added several weighty stones to the bag's gruesome contents and flung it far out into the dark depths. Returning, he scoured the kennel free of all traces of blood. Then he went into the kitchen where his mother and Carl sat at the breakfast table with the remainder of the family.

'How's the dog?' his mother asked.

'He seems to have run away,' Wally answered.

'Run away?' his mother echoed. 'Why would he run away?'

'Don't know,' Wally returned, 'all I know is he's gone.'

'Would he have been stolen?' his mother asked.

'It's a possibility,' Wally told her.

At that moment Carl arose and without a word left the kitchen. His sudden action made everything clear to Maisie Hern.

Shortly afterwards Carl sold the white dog to a local trainer. As if by agreement there was no mention of either dog in the Hern home after that. The people of the locality accepted the black dog's disappearance at face value. It certainly wasn't the first time a promising greyhound had been stolen and it wouldn't be the last. It was around this time that Wally decided he would have to leave home. It wasn't just the incident of

the butchered greyhound. This was only one of many decid-
ing factors, the chief of which was Carl's sudden obsession
with any girl Wally might take it into his head to court. Carl
simply had to have her as well but not all of Wally's dates were
willing to co-operate. When this happened Carl would fly into
a rage and frighten the girl in question. In so doing he also
queered the pitch for Wally.

The girls might be forgiven for concluding that, because
he was a twin, Wally was just as likely to explode into a tan-
trum as his brother. He knew that he would always be in danger of being tarred with the same brush unless he made the
break. He discussed every aspect of the matter with his mother. She was forced to concede that there was no other course
open to him. He promised to return for good some day but
this was not his intention. He wanted to get as far away from
Carl as possible and to stay away so that he might build an
independent and natural life for himself. London he believed
would afford him the anonymity he desired. Nobody would
ever find him there. He would miss his mother and his younger brothers and sisters and, of course, Carl.

Despite the envy and the resentment he loved his twin
more than any other member of the family, his mother except-
ed. He would keep in touch with all of them but he would not
reveal his address. He would send his mother money on a regular basis and he would bring her for a holiday occasionally
but the life he would begin in the city would be strictly his
own.

It wasn't long before he invested in an ancient house in
south-east London. In his spare time he restored it to its original appearance. The area he chose was singularly free of Irish

emigrants. He didn't want anybody returning home with word of his whereabouts until his relationship with Carl assumed reasonable proportions. This might never happen but he dared to hope that one day it would. Until such time, however, as he could be absolutely certain that a normal relationship was assured he would keep the location of his house a secret. Then he met Sally. She was a midlander several years younger than he. After a brief courtship they married secretly. After awhile, at Sally's insistence, Wally let his family know that he had taken a wife. He promised to bring her on a visit as soon as possible. Two years were to pass before he decided to present her to Maisie and the family.

Sally knew all about Carl. Wally had told her everything. Mercifully Carl accepted her as a member of the family. He too had married a few months previously and was, according to himself, as happy as any man could wish to be. There followed a wonderful holiday. Wally was amazed at the change which had come over Carl. He seemed to have recognised that he no longer had anything to be jealous about. His wife was a vivacious and lovely girl, far more attractive than Sally, highly desirable in every possible way. No man could wish for more in a girl. He had set up his own plumbing business and there was wide demand for his services. It seemed that in Wally's absence he had given his true character a chance to develop. Financially he was far better off than Wally who, after all, was only a clog in a wheel and hadn't the sort of initiative or drive to start off on his own. He would always be content working for somebody else.

Carl owned a bigger car, a bigger house. If he compared his lot with Wally's and it was highly unlikely that he was any longer given to such a purposeless practice, there would have to be a glow of satisfaction when he considered his position.

When, on the eve of Wally's departure, Carl asked him if he could help him in any way, financially or otherwise, Wally's last remaining reservations vanished and he knew he no longer had anything to fear from his twin.

Wally thanked him profusely for the offer of assistance but declined on the grounds that he already had all he wanted. No sooner had he said this, however, then he realised that he might be giving Carl food for thought. He realised that to suggest he had everything he could possibly want was a mistake. It was possible that Carl might not have everything he could possibly want so to place himself at a disadvantage he asked Carl for a loan of twenty pounds until he got back to London. Carl was delighted to hand over the money and suggested that Wally keep it as a belated wedding present. Wally agreed to this. For the first time in his life Wally really knew what freedom meant. Always at the back of his mind while he was in London had been the fear that Carl might show up and wreck everything. That was all behind him now and he could breathe easily. He could also go where he liked in London and renew old friendships with other exiles.

At the end of four years of marriage neither twin was blessed with issue although there had been assurances from both family doctors that there was no apparent reason why this should be so. About this time Carl and his wife took a holiday in London. They stayed with Wally and Sally both of whom took a week off from work so as to be fully at the disposal of their guests.

It was a week of non-stop activity. If Carl had accumulated a great deal of money it wasn't because he was miserly. He spent prodigally throughout the week. When, at the end they left for home exhausted but happy, Carl declared that it was the most wonderful week of his entire life. For Wally it was much more. The normal brotherly relationship for which he had wished so devoutly for so long had manifested itself unmistakably for the length of the holiday. He began to experience a contentment and sense of fulfilment which brought a totally new dimension of bliss into his life. The ominous shadows which had hovered over his deepest thoughts up until this time were now irrevocably dispersed and had been replaced by an almost dizzying feeling of release. There were times when he suffered fleeting pangs of guilt so rich and full was his new-found situation. He resolved to adopt a truly charitable and selfless approach to life in return for the great favour which had been bestowed upon him. He no longer recalled the hideous events of the past nor feared in the slightest for the future. He relayed his feelings to Sally and she in turn revealed that she also felt a sense of relief.

Around this time Wally's firm secured an overseas contract as a result of which he would have to spend at least three weeks abroad. There was simply no opting out. If he were to decide in favour of such a course he could easily find himself looking for a new job. Sally assured him that she would be all right. She had her job and after all what were three weeks in a lifetime! The last of his reservations disappeared when she said that one of the girls in the office had volunteered to stay with her until he returned home. At the airport just before his departure he found himself quite overcome by a nauseating feeling of loneliness. It was as unexpected as it was painful.

'I didn't realise it would be like this,' he told Sally who had taken a half day off from work to drive him to the airport.

'It's only three weeks,' she consoled.

'But I'll be so far away from you. Equador's almost half-way round the world.'

'Look,' Sally laid her hand on his arm, 'you don't have to go. It isn't as if we need the money and besides you can always get another job.'

'Too late for that now,' he said. 'I couldn't very well back out at this stage. They'd never find a replacement at such short notice. Then there are my mates. No! I have to go. It's as simple as that. I don't want to but something tells me I'd feel a lot lousier if I stayed behind.'

'It will be worth it all when you come home to me,' she whispered.

They kissed and he held her briefly in his arms. He released her without a word and walked off hurriedly to the departure area. She stood unmoving for a long while before turning towards the car park.

In Equador Wally lost himself in his work. Because of labour difficulties the job took longer than was anticipated. At night he wrote long letters to Sally. In these he told her how much he longed to be home and how much he pined for her. He received several letters in return but they arrived weeks late so that he could only guess at the existing situation. The letters were full of warmth and concern for him. Finally the contract was fulfilled and the time came to return home. He sent a telegram from Guayaquel indicating the approximate time of his homecoming. Because of various delays it took two days to complete the journey.

Exhausted but elated he set foot on English soil at eight o'clock in the morning. Immediately he hastened to the nearest phone booth. Sally never left for work before eight forty-five. He would have no difficulty in making contact with her. In the booth his heart fluttered in anticipation. He longed with all his heart to hear the sound of her voice. He was surprised and disappointed when she did not respond. The phone was ringing all right but nobody came to answer. He was not unduly alarmed. There had been mornings when she was forced to dash for work without breakfast. It was, therefore, quite possible that she was still slumbering. He smiled fondly at the thought of her lying beyond her time in their comfortable double bed. He replaced the receiver and left the booth. After a cup of coffee and a sandwich he decided to make a second call. He looked at his watch. There was still time enough to catch her before she left for work. Still the same mechanical response. He laid down the receiver, bitterly disappointed.

In the taxi he comforted himself with the thought that she had probably slept it out altogether. This had happened on one or two occasions when he had been away overnight on the firm's business. He could think of no other reason unless she had been taken ill. In this unlikely but remotely possible circumstance she would have gone to her parents home outside Northampton. He ordered the driver to pull up at the nearest phone booth. It was Sally's mother who answered the call. No. Sally was not with them. The last time she had heard from her was three weeks before. She had sounded all right then. He told his mother-in-law about the calls. She advised him not to worry. Sally was certainly at home asleep in her bed. Where else could she be? He made a third call to his home but there was no reply.

As they drove through the empty streets the first feelings of disquiet began to assail him. He asked himself a number of questions. Where, for instance, was the girl who was supposed to be staying with Sally during his absence? Surely one of the two should have heard the phone ringing and answered it! Where could Sally be if she wasn't in her own or her parents' home? Why was she not on the alert when she knew approximately the time he would be arriving? There could only be one possible answer. She had slept it out. But what if she had not? What if she hadn't slept at home the night before or on previous nights?

All sorts of terrible conclusions entered his mind. The most dreadful of all he dared not contemplate. As the taxi neared its destination he grew more apprehensive until finally he reached a state where he dreaded the prospect of entering the house. Almost at once he chided himself for his lack of faith in a woman who had all her married life been an exemplary spouse. There had to be a perfect explanation for the lack of response to his calls.

When, at length, the taxi-driver deposited him at his front door he hesitated. He fumbled for his key and located it. He was about to insert it in the lock but he changed his mind and rang the doorbell instead. He waited a full minute before ringing a second time. The second summons proved as futile as the first. He inserted the key and entered the hallway. Her name was on his lips but no sound came. Slowly he climbed the stairs to the bedroom they had shared for the past four years. The bed was empty, the room deserted. There was still the possibility, of course, that she might have just vacated the house in a scramble to reach the office on time. He decided to ring the office. After a short wait he was put through to her supervisor. His wife had not been in all week nor had she made any form of contact. The last time the supervisor had seen her had been the previous Friday afternoon. It was now Thursday. No. She could offer no explanation nor had she any idea of her whereabouts. He asked if he might speak to the girl who had elected to stay with Sally during his absence. She came on the line at once. Yes. She had stayed for the required period. She presumed that he had returned when he said he would. Sally had made no mention of an extension of the contract. He replaced the phone and sat on the stairs. Suddenly he became violently sick. He staggered into the kitchen for a cloth with which to clean the area where he had vomited.

The sheet of note paper was pinned prominently to the kitchen cabinet directly over the sink. Despairingly he forced himself to read it. There wasn't much. It was signed Sally. It said: 'Gone with Carl. Sorry.'

All the old depressions which he had experienced since childhood came flooding back. He sat on a chair and started to sob uncontrollably. He crumpled the sheet in his hand and flung it at the far wall. It bounced on the tiled floor and landed at his feet. He became sick a second time. Afterwards he went upstairs and lay on the bed. Wave after wave of total despair engulfed him until he was all but suffocated. He had never felt so despondent in his life. What had happened was the culmination of all the worst fantasies he had ever experienced, the ultimate in sheer human hopelessness. He cursed himself for having ever left for Equador. He should have known that what had happened was always well within the

178

bounds of possibility provided the proper set of circumstances presented themselves at a given time. He could not find it in his heart to blame Sally. He saw her role as inevitable, as a necessary part of his destiny. He lay in bed all day but even after several hours he was still badly stunned by the shock of her departure. He tossed and turned until, from sheer force of fatigue, he fell into an uneasy sleep. When he awakened the phone was ringing. He rushed to answer it. His mother's voice greeted him. At once he burst into tears. She had guessed the worst when Carl had disappeared without warning the week before. She had known for some time of Wally's impending trip overseas and so had Carl. It required no great detective work on her part when Carl's wife arrived at the door in a distraught state a few days after he had gone off without warning. Wally was glad when his mother informed him that she intended to spend some time with him.

She arrived the following evening and stayed for a month. Anxiously she listened as he moved about the house long after she had gone to bed. Always it would be well into the morning before he eventually retired. Even then it was doubtful if he slept. His eyes were bloodshot in the mornings. He found it as much as he could do to drag himself to his place of employment.

For the first few days after his homecoming he had absented himself from work but the days had proved too long and dismal and it seemed that they would never pass. He decided to return to work. It was better than mooning around the house where everything he touched reminded him of his absent wife. The weeks passed but no word came. Every so often he would ring her parents' home in the hope that they might have heard something. It was always a fruitless exercise.

Towards the end of the fourth week his sleep returned and so did his appetite. His mother was grateful for these symptoms of a return to some sort of normalcy. She told him that she had overstayed her leave and he accepted this. She bade him a tearful goodbye promising to return at once should he relapse into his earlier despondency. Carl's wife recovered from the loss and the shock at the end of the second day. She flung herself whole-heartedly into the business which she had helped her husband establish. The employees, instead of resenting a female at the helm, became her devoted followers and worked harder than ever to ensure that she should succeed. She played every card at her disposal, using every womanly wile with workforce and customers alike. Her desire to succeed was exceeded only by her hatred of her husband. She was determined never to forgive him. Let him return if he wished one day and he would find his business at least as successful as he had left it but he would find her as cold as stone. In this her resolve was rigid. It was the sheer detestation of him that kept her going during the first difficult weeks while she endeavoured to acquire a working knowledge of the business.

She felt no sorrow for Wally. He was after all the twin brother of the man who had forsaken her and what sort of witless weakling was he, she asked herself, that couldn't hold on to his plain Jane of a wife! She had little sympathy for Maisie Hern either. She found her guilty by association. By dint of hard work she would erase the memory of her husband. By ploughing a lone furrow she would become independent of him until one day he would cease to be an impression on her lifestyle. She knew she would succeed in this. It made her work, hard and demanding as it was, enjoyable and satisfying. She would be self-sufficient no matter what. This was the goal that sustained her.

Six months were to pass before Wally Hern found himself responding rationally to the life around him. The grief remained but it was now in a secondary stage, less painful although no less lonely than the first. It was a change from the all-consuming heartache of the first months.

His mother revisited him for a few days the following spring. She found him haggard in appearance but otherwise healthy. He stayed up late and rose early but there was none of the fretful pacing of the first visit. Her concern for him kept her awake into the small hours. Of all her children he deserved to be hurt the least. Repeatedly she asked herself how they had reached such a dilemma. Carl's envy was the obvious answer but it wasn't as simple as that. If her husband had played his rightful role they might never have found themselves in this deadly predicament. Typically, she refused to absolve her daughters-in-law, particularly Carl's wife, whose initiative she interpreted as downright bitchiness. She could not or would not blame herself. She had done her utmost. Granted, this was not enough but no mother in a similar set of circumstances could have done more. She left for home after three days. Wally promised faithfully he would spend the summer holidays with her. She knew, however, that he would never leave the house, not even for a day, while there remained the faintest hope that his wife would return.

Sally returned on Christmas Eve after an absence of fifteen

months. Using her key she let herself in silently and stood in the hallway not daring to go further. Wally knew from the un-expected draught that the front door had been opened. Only one other person had a key. He rose unsteadily from his chair, his heart thumping, not daring to believe that she might have returned. Mustering his courage he opened the kitchen door and saw her standing there.

'Happy Christmas,' he managed to get the words out. He took her in his arms, smothering the apologies that sprung to her lips with loving fingers. Later, after they had made love, no matter how hard she tried he would not allow her utter a self-condemnatory word. For the first time since her absence he slept deeply. The morning after he did not awaken till shortly before noon.

'We'll have to talk,' Sally said after they had breakfast.

'There's no need,' he told her. 'All that matters is that you're back.'

He steadfastly refused to hear any sort of explanation, reassuring her with kisses every time she tried to start. That night Carl arrived. Wally it was who answered the door. Carl brushed past him silently and went straight to the kitchen where he confronted Sally. Ignoring Wally, who had followed him, he pushed her on to a chair.

'Why couldn't you have told me?' he glowered down at her at though he were about to strike her. His hands hung by his sides, his fists clenched. 'Why did you sneak off like that?' he demanded.

'Watch how you talk to my wife,' Wally spoke menacing-ly.

Carl turned on him and spat on the floor at his feet.

'Your wife,' he scoffed, 'your wife indeed. I'm not talking to your wife brother dear. I am talking to my woman!'

He made every word sound more loathsome than the next. He raised an arm aloft but Wally seized him by both hands and held him in a vice-like grip. He forced him on to a chair. Carl fumed and ranted but he was powerless to move.

'You're leaving here now and you'll never return,' Wally told him. 'All my life you've wanted anything of value I ever owned, my dog, my peace of mind, my standing, my wife. There's an end to it now. You can take no more from me.'

'I can take your life,' Carl spat back at him.

'Be careful,' Wally warned, 'that I don't take yours.'

Releasing him he put an arm around Sally.

'Just walk out that door and go about your business. Let me to mine from this night out or you'll be sorry. Go now and a happy Christmas to you.'

Carl rose and addressed himself to Sally.

'Look me in the face,' he screamed. 'Look in my eyes and tell me I must leave.'

Slowly she raised her head until her gaze was level with his. She spoke calmly and unwaveringly. 'This is my husband,' she said 'and this is my home.'

'Is it?' he asked, his face distorted with rage. 'Suppose I tell him what you've been to me, what we've been through together. You have no more right to this home anymore than you have to him. You gave yourself to me willingly or was it a whore I held in my arms? Was it a whore? Answer me and I'll leave peacefully.'

'Say another word to her and I'll smash your face in,' Wally cautioned.

'Are you afraid to let her answer,' Carl taunted.

'You were warned,' Wally cried hoarsely as he smashed a mighty fist into his brother's face. Carl fell to the floor. Wally stood towering over him ready to knock him down again. The gun appeared as if by magic in Carl's right hand. Wally stood paralysed. He had never looked into the barrel of a gun before. On Carl's face was a look which sent the cold terror running through him. The finality in his brother's eyes was terrifying to behold. Suddenly Wally knew how it was going to end. He lunged forward in a despairing effort to restrain him but even as he moved Carl had turned the gun inward towards himself and fired it into his breast. The gun fell from his hand. The blood gushed outward in a spate as the force of the blast threw him backwards on the floor. Death came instantly. Wally knew the moment he lifted his brother's head that life had departed. Death had also removed the snarl from Carl's face and replaced it with a look of serenity that Wally had never before seen there. It was as though he had finally resolved the terrible enigma which had tormented him all his life.

THE URGING
OF
CHRISTMAS

YOU CAN'T POSTPONE THE TRUE URGING OF Christmas. You have to do it now. That's the acid test of the man who would be Christmas. If you're a drinking man go and have a drink and it will help you do the right thing. Even a roasting fire won't thaw a frozen heart but a glass of whiskey might. I've seen it happen.

I've also seen Christmas destroyed by whiskey for whiskey is a dangerous cargo without plimsoll line or compass. It must be treated as if it were dynamite.

Then on the other hand, imbued by the spirit of Christmas and a bellyful of booze, I beheld a man who normally would not give you the itch lift his phone and beg his estranged daughter to come home for Christmas. She came with a heart and a half and on both sides all was forgiven. He wasn't half as mean thereafter. So, my friends, taking Christmas by the horns can work wonders.

Don't ever be ashamed to be weepy or sentimental about Christmas because you might not get the chance during the year ahead to show your humanity to the world and what the

185

hell good is humanity if it's suffocated by caution! That's what Christmas is for, taking from our natural stock of humanity and disbursing it where it will do the most good.

If you have to think twice about the impulses that move you to be forgiving and charitable and loving you'll miss the boat. Generosity diminishes the more one considers it. The milk of human kindness doesn't come from cows or goats. It comes from the human heart, that great institute of compassion and repository of human hope.

If a man only submitted himself once a year to the dictates of Christmas all would not be lost but we have some who acknowledge the birth of Christ by regarding it as a day, the same as any other, when they may kill and maim at will. However, no matter what they do, the spirit of Christmas will survive and they will be long forgotten.

The spirit of Christmas has survived the Stalins, the Hitlers and the Mussolinis and all those too who have perpetrated injustices since the birth of Christ. It has survived human greed and human jealousy and every human failing one cares to mention.

All the moons that have waxed and waned since the birth of Christ will testify that nothing lasts like Christmas. Not all the inhumanity, nor all the greed, nor all the violence will reduce its message by a whit. It's here to stay and there's nothing that evil men can do about it and that's one great consolation.

Officially declaring Christmas non-existent can work only for a while. You can't keep Christmas down for long. It is the most buoyant of all festivals.

There are ways, of course, of destroying the Christmases

of individuals, of families and of communities and the chief of these is to drive while you're drunk. You may drink after you drive but never before.

Just say to yourself: 'I'll enjoy a few Christmas drinks when I arrive at my destination but not before. This will be my Christmas gift to my fellow man.'

You can start a row in a pub or a hotel and upset the Christmases of legitimate workers who have enough to contend with during anti-social hours. You can upset your home and your family by being too drunk or too mean or too intolerant or, worst of all, by being indifferent.

These are but a few. There are so many more. However, I know in my heart that you, dear reader, will do none of those heinous things. You'll try to do otherwise. Just try and since God loves a trier you're halfway there already.

Don't think I'm pontificating. I'm not. I'm trying to explain what Christmas should be all about. It's a time of opportunity. The climate is perfect for revealing our better natures. Just as the spring assures growth of crops so does Christmas assure growth of love.

It is not possible for man, because of his very nature, to be charitable and compassionate all the year round. Let us, therefore, make the most of Christmas.

> *Heap on more wood! the wind is chill;*
> *But let it whistle as it will.*
> *We'll keep our Christmas merry still.*

So wrote the great Walter Scott long before Dickens wrote *A Christmas Carol* which gives the lie to those who would say that Dickens invented Christmas as we know it. Christmas was never invented. It was born out of love and carries on out of love.

I once asked an old woman what she would do if there was no Christmas.

'I don't know,' she said, 'but I wouldn't be bothered with anything else.'

Personally speaking, I don't know how I would survive if Christmas were to be abolished. There would be no point in getting drunk because that would only remind me of Christmas all the more.

I could not imagine a more bleak world. I just cannot conceive anything of commensurate magnitude to replace it. We should, therefore, be down on our knees thanking God that it is there.

If there was no Christmas there would be no *Adeste*, no *Silent Night*, no carol singing, no Santa Claus. I could go on and on. There would be nothing without Christmas because it's the plinth on which the rest of the year stands.

Sometime when you are alone with nothing to do try to remember all the things that would never again be if we lost Christmas. There is nothing else with the power to move the human heart to its utmost capability. For God's sake don't take it for granted. If you haven't done anything about it yet for pity's sake do it now or you'll be guilty of the awful crime of trying to undermine Christmas.